Nick sudde... laughed lightly.

"I'm giving you a hard time, Kristen, aren't I?"

She watched him as he stood up and came over to where she was sitting. When he took her hand and pulled her up beside him, they were standing very close together and Kristen was shocked and disgusted with herself to discover that his touch was like an electric shock. She felt overpowered, and when he put his arms around her and traced her spine with his fingers, she found herself holding her breath, her eyes clinging to his.

After a moment he said very softly, "You've been so nice to my aunt, why not be nice to me? You never know, it might pay off, too."

"What are you saying to me?" Kristen asked in a stifled voice.

"You intrigue me," he told her, "and I happen to want you—very much."

Wynne May was born near Johannesburg, South Africa. Shortly after graduating from college, she began working for the South African Broadcasting Corporation. While on holiday she met Claude, the handsome green-eyed stranger who spoke to her after she slipped and fell into a swimming pool! Three months later Claude slipped a diamond ring onto Wynne's finger as they stood under the stars in an exotic garden. Wynne now spends her time with her family—and writing romances.

Books by Wynne May

A Flaunting Cactus

Wynne May

Harlequin Books

TORONTO • NEW YORK • LONDON
AMSTERDAM • PARIS • SYDNEY • HAMBURG
STOCKHOLM • ATHENS • TOKYO • MILAN

Original hardcover edition published in 1986
by Mills & Boon Limited

ISBN 0-373-17016-5

Harlequin Romance first edition June 1988

CHAPTER ONE

KRISTEN Ashton's unusual golden-green eyes were moody and she felt a wreck. Dining, on Christmas Eve, with Miss Elizabeth Lathbury—who had been nicknamed Holly as a girl—was proving to be a disaster.

Holly was an attractive and sophisticated woman in her middle sixties, and at present her face was a mask of contempt. One hand went to her sleekly drawn-back silver hair, before straying to a necklace of gold chains and rhinestones.

'I knew, from the beginning,' she was saying, 'that this Ferdi Jaeger is not the man for you—and what's more, Kristen, I knew he wouldn't keep his promise to you, and I was right, wasn't I? Back for Christmas, indeed! He's probably met a girl in Gstaad. Do you imagine for one moment that he's being faithful to you? I know these Alpine resorts. Your engagement is heading one way, and that's my candid opinion!'

Listening to Holly, Kristen felt frustrated and abandoned by Ferdi, but, trying to keep her feelings from showing, she said mildly, 'He probably decided to stay on—at the last moment.'

Since moving into the flat, which formed part of Holly's Colonial mansion high on the Berea and overlooking the Indian Ocean, she had reached the conclusion that her wealthy landlady was rather eccentric. It had all started promisingly, but Holly's often meddlesome ways, although usually innocent enough, and her overwhelming generosity, were

5

beginning to give rise for concern. Holly's outlook on life was, no doubt, embittered by the fact that, as a young woman, she had been let down—almost at the altar.

'I'll tell you why he's changed his mind, Kristen. It's not the glittering Alpine slopes he's concerned about, it's some girl. You mark my words!'

During the seemingly never-ending meal in the huge antique-filled dining-room with its high ceiling, gleaming floor and magnificent Persian rugs, nephew Nick Lathbury's fiancée, Barbro, also came under the whip.

'The nerve of that girl never fails to astound me,' Holly went on, while Kristen made a big pretence of enjoying her dinner. 'She goes out of her way to point out that this glorious site, with its Indian Ocean views, is ideal for town houses. Imagine! A rash of hideous town houses on this old historical site? Let me tell you, this is a house with a history, and it's one of Durban's gracious old homes. Corporation records disclose the property in the 1888 valuation roll as belonging to Captain Paul Lathbury. Now do you understand why I'm so furious? Those converted lamps outside are the only reminders of days gone by. Gone are the carriage-and-pair . . . gone, and probably forgotten, unless you happen to be a Lathbury! Well, I am a Lathbury, and Nick is a Lathbury. I've shown you the look-out on the top of one wing of the house, Kristen, and I've explained that it was used to watch the arrival of ships. The telescope and flag are both still there, to this day, and both serve to remind one of the exchange of signals with vessels as they entered the harbour.'

Kristen's thoughts went to the day when, refusing

help, Holly had climbed the ladder from the attic to the look-out while she had watched from below. As Holly had pushed back a trapdoor and begun to ease herself up, she had called down impatiently, 'Well, come on, child. Just follow me up.'

Holly's voice continued to drone on. 'Town houses here? Over my dead body!'

'You shouldn't be brooding on these things,' Kristen answered. 'You just make yourself unhappy.'

'Would *you* like to see town houses replace this mansion?' Holly's fingers wrapped themseles around the gold chains and rhinestones.

'No, of course not!' Without her intending it, Kristen's voice had risen. 'I'd hate to see that, but——'

'Well, there you are then. You have a sensitivity about the things that matter,' Holly replied.

In an effort to curb these unwelcome confidences, Kristen tried to change the subject. 'What about gravy, Holly?'

'I have gravy,' Holly snapped. 'To get back to this girl. She's not the girl I'd choose for Nick.'

Without appearing to think what she was doing, Holly poured herself another glass of red wine. She had also indulged in two Bloody Marys before dinner, which was surprising, as, apart from a little wine on special occasions, she did not drink.

'Perhaps you're misunderstanding Barbro,' Kristen began, but Holly cut in quickly.

'Have *you* met her?' Her blue eyes were blazing.

'No, Holly, I haven't, but——'

'Exactly. Now tell me, looking at that so-called Christmas card, would you still say I'm mis-understanding her?' Holly pushed back her chair and stood up, and Kristen watched her with dismay, as she went to retrieve Barbro's hand-crafted Christmas card from the long sideboard.

'Take another look at this.' Holly almost flung the card on the table. 'I've told you she's a graphic designer. She thinks *that* makes her an architect, by the way. When she designed this card, she designed it with the intention of infuriating me, and she has. Did she think I wouldn't recognise my own flame tree in the picture she's drawn? She has also gone to considerable length to draw the Christmas tree in the garden and she's cunningly festooned it with coloured lights, and what does it all add up to? These two trees, which have been on the site for years and years, flank a rash of Mediterranean-influenced town houses, all with ridiculous balconies set behind white holes in the walls. Don't tell me you don't recognise that car, either—wrapped as it is in ribbons. That's my 1938 Morris Eight. Is it—or is it not?'

'Perhaps it was just done to tease you, Holly.' Kristen, brooding on her own troubles, felt like shrieking.

'Tease me? Let me tell you something. Barbro is just dying to get her hands on that car—something about shocking the male chauvinists, I believe. Chauvinists! We never gave *that one* a thought, in my day. Well, directly I received the card I went to Frank Prentice, my lawyer, and I had him change my Will. That alone caused me to lose my temper, because Frank did nothing but argue with me. It's *my* Will, after all! After that, I went to the flat Barbro shares with another so-called liberated young woman, and I had much relish in passing on my news.' Holly lowered her voice to a conspiratorial tone. 'In view of the fact that Nick is going to marry Barbro, he no longer stands to inherit this house, or the car. I actually saw her face pale.'

'You shouldn't be telling me all this,' Kristen said angrily. 'Don't you feel bad? You should do, you know.'

'I don't feel in the least bad.' Holly spread ringed fingers. 'After all, Nick is a very wealthy young man. He inherited Lathbury Interiors from his father—and he was just a child at the time—but it was all tied up, of course, until the right time. He owns a Jaguar—well, you've seen it. Micky's taking care of it, while Nick is overseas. No, Kristen. By changing my Will I believe I have safeguarded this property, and all it stands for, from the future Mrs Nicholas Lathbury.'

'You shouldn't be discussing Wills, especially over Christmas.' Kristen shook her head. 'It's ugly, Holly, and it's terribly morbid. Especially, though, you shouldn't be discussing your private affairs with me. After all, until only a matter of three months ago I was completely unknown to you. Right?'

'Kristen, I've known you long enough to realise that I can trust you, believe me.'

Listening to all this, Kristen began to ask herself whether she had done the right thing in accepting Holly's offer of the flat.

'Holly,' she said, after a moment, 'you're really being very naughty, you know. Isn't it silly to be drinking quite so much when you're not used to it?'

'If I'm drinking too much it's because I have problems,' Holly snapped. 'Haven't I just spent the last half-hour trying to explain them to you? Even telling you about Frank, who had the audacity to dispute my Will. How do you think I felt about that, Kristen?'

'You've had a lot of wine,' Kristen went on, 'and you downed two vodkas before dinner.'

'Well, I just feel like breaking out for once in my life—and, talking about breaking out, we should have gone out to dinner. I don't know why I didn't think of it. We should have reserved a table at some plush hotel on the beachfront. After all, we're both miserable, and it does happen to be Christmas Eve. I'm so cross with Nick. He wrote to say he'd be back in time for Christmas Day, *at least*. He went to some length to explain that he'd come to the end of his extended business trip in London but that he was taking the chance to go to Scotland for four or five days, after which he'd take the first available flight home. It's understandable, I think, that I should be feeling just a little put out. Nick is the son I never had, and, what's more, we form the entire family.'

'Well, something must have delayed him,' Kristen murmured, but she was thinking, You've told me these things over and over again, Holly, and I feel like screaming! 'Perhaps he couldn't get a seat on the plane when he wanted one. I mean, that makes sense. He'd never do this on purpose.'

The outcome of the dinner was that Holly retired long before midnight, leaving Kristen feeling tired and depressed. After clearing up and blowing out the candles on the long, gleaming table, she turned off the coloured lights on the ceiling-high Christmas tree (Holly had a standing order for one, every year) which stood in the formal drawing-room, and went along to her own flat, where she tried to take her mind off Ferdi by reading.

After several minutes, she put the book down and found herself brooding on her brother Craig, who was now married to Libby and living in Cape Town, having been promoted there by his firm. Kristen and Craig had shared a flat, but most of the furniture had belonged to her and she had brought everything along to her present flat and was thrilled at the way in which it had fitted in.

It was strange what furniture could do, she thought. Holly's part of the house was almost oppressive with its antiques, Persian rugs, oil paintings in ornate gilt frames and priceless accessories—mostly all inherited, Holly had explained repeatedly, along with the 1938 Morris Eight car. Poor old Morris, it seemed to be at the back of everything, and it was due to it that she was now renting the flat from Holly.

Craig had admired the Morris at the garage where he and Micky Naidoo had been buying petrol and Craig had mentioned that he would give anything to hire a car like it, on the occasion of his forthcoming marriage. Interested in photography, Craig had visions of the exciting photo album which would record that perfect day. Micky had then suggested that Craig should speak to Miss Elizabeth Lathbury. 'On Fridays,' he had said, according to Craig, 'I always drive her to her Garden Club, but I fill the car with petrol first—ready for the weekend, in case she wants to go somewhere. I'm sure, if you spoke to her, she wouldn't mind letting you use the car, especially if there's a photo in the newspaper.'

Thanks to Micky Naidoo, the rest had followed. Holly had been thrilled to have the happy couple use her treasured car. The only thing she had asked was that Micky should drive the car. Having been jilted— her word—she had refused to attend the wedding, however. A friendship developed between the young couple concerned, not to mention with Kristen.

Looking back to that day, not so long ago, Kristen sighed sleepily. Nicholas Lathbury had already left on his extended business trip but, according to Holly, he knew about the wedding and the loan of her car, because she had sent him a cutting of the newspaper.

Soon after Craig's wedding Em, Holly's friend, had gone to live with her daughter and the flat which had been created from one wing of Holly's mansion was unoccupied and, in view of the fact that Kristen was flat-hunting, Holly had immediately offered her Em's flat, which she gratefully accepted.

The flat was now a reflection of Kristen's own taste. There were books and flowers and plants everywhere and, apart from the gleaming yellow-wood furniture which Holly had asked her to store in the flat, her own furniture was modern and comfortable and looked expensive—but wasn't. Two plump and deep off-white sofas were cushion-piled in such vibrant colours as coral, peacock-blue and lime-green and looked perfect against the pale coral walls and white-painted doors and skirtings. Before Kristen had taken over the flat the walls had been beige to suit Em, who had lived in the flat for several years, but Holly had insisted that Kristen should choose her own colour-scheme, and after the flat had been painted, Kristen had moved in. Because it was part of a gracious house it was a flat with a difference. Tall French doors with freshly painted frames around small panes of glass punctuated one entire wall of the sitting-room and there were attractive lamps, bowls of flowers and a few carefully chosen ornaments. The coffee-table was large and glass-topped and potted plants with shining, dark green leaves, the colour of Nick Lathbury's beautiful

Jaguar, had been placed at various points where they could catch the lamplight by night and the sunlight during the day. The plants had been gifts from Holly and had come from the garden.

Kristen was almost asleep, on the sofa, when the shrieking of a phone disturbed her and, confused at first, she looked at the ivory-and-gold telephone which stood on Holly's yellow-wood chest of drawers in the small hallway which was separated from the sitting-room by means of a wide, white-pillared archway. The sound was not coming from there. She realised that the phone was ringing in Holly's part of the house, nevertheless her thoughts flew immediately to Ferdi. He had phoned! Ferdi had phoned!

Struggling up, she ran to the entrance-hall and made her way into a small corridor where there was a door which always remained unlocked and which was used at night if she had been watching television with Holly. It was a door to use in the case of an emergency—and this was an emergency, for she was quite sure that Ferdi had forgotten her telephone number but had found out the listed Lathbury number.

Lifting the receiver, she said, 'Hello?' She realised she was shaking. 'Ferdi, darling, is that you?'

The silence at the other end was brief and then a man's voice said, 'Not Ferdi. Sorry to disappoint you, but this is Nick, Nick Lathbury—and you sound like Kristen.'

Kristen felt a great wave of disappointment wash over her. The voice at the other end of the line might just as well have said, 'This is Bond. James Bond.'

After a moment of readjusting she said, 'Yes, it is Kristen. I'm sorry, but your aunt is in bed. I'm afraid she's had rather too much to drink. I doubt if I could wake her, right now.'

She heard him laugh and then he said, 'Are you kidding?'

'No, I'm not.' Thinking about Ferdi made her voice suddenly waspish.

'And who is driving my aunt to drink?' he asked, and she could hear the smile in his voice. 'You?'

'No, *you're* responsible for that. She was absolutely wretched this evening. She's been expecting you back for the past three days. I mean,' she lifted her shoulders, 'England is a long way off, and in case you've forgotten, it does just happen to be Christmas Eve.' Her tone was accusing but the jibe was really being aimed—uselessly—at Ferdi.

'I'm not so far away,' Nick Lathbury said easily. 'I'm at the airport.'

Kristen stiffened. 'The airport? You mean *our* airport?'

The fact that it was Nicholas Lathbury's voice, and not Ferdi's, had disappointed her and unlocked all the pent-up feelings in her, and with her free hand she wiped the tears from her cheeks.

'Yes, our airport. I wanted to let Holly know that I've arrived. The plane was delayed at Harare for eleven hours and at this time of night I can't get a taxi from here. I'm about to phone for an all-night taxi from Durban—unless,' he laughed lightly, 'you want to come for me?'

She remained silent and then she heard him say, 'Well, how about it—or have *you* had too much to drink?'

'No, I haven't. At least—I haven't had much. I had dinner with Holly.'

'Did I wake you?' he asked.

'No, I was reading.' She had seen a black and white photo of Nick, and since she had never met him, she now tried to conjure up this image.

'How about taking pity on a weary traveller?' he went on. 'I understand you're a very successful young lady with her own red Mazda.'

Holly must have been busy with her pen, Kristen found herself thinking.

'So? When can I expect you, Kristen?' he asked.

'I didn't say I was coming,' she answered stiffly.

'Is that an answer?'

After a moment, out of sheer boredom and depression, she said, 'All right, I'll come. Give me say—twenty minutes.'

'You're a star,' he said lightly. 'I'll be outside International Arrivals and, according to Holly's description, I'll be on the look out for a girl with dark red hair and green eyes.'

Kristen heard the phone go down at the other end and taking the receiver from her ear she stared at it for a moment. 'I don't believe this,' she said, aloud. 'Why did you have to go and say you'd pick him up, you stupid mutt?'

To curb her ruffled feelings she tried not to hurry. Let him wait, she thought, like he's kept Holly waiting until the last minute—like Ferdi's keeping me waiting.

When she had applied a little fresh make-up and combed her hair she went outside, discovered that it had started to rain and went back into her flat to fetch a raincoat, which she flung on to the back seat of the car.

The breeze had cleared her head, but as she drove to the airport her thoughts were confused and revolved around Ferdi, who had not even bothered to write.

Heavy drops of rain began to fall, slanting over the car, and in between the sweeping movements of the wipers, they blurred the windscreen.

Nick Lathbury was waiting outside International Arrivals, and drawing level with him, Kristen reached across the seat, rolled down the window and watched him as he came over to her. Her spectacular golden-green eyes were wide as he stooped to look into the car and in the yellow glow from the building behind him she could see that his eyes were a deep blue. The black and white photo which Holly had shown her had not prepared her for Nick's exciting good looks, and she felt a thud in her stomach.

For the briefest instant, their eyes locked and then he smiled, showing a groove in one cheek. 'Holly forgot to mention that you had the look of a jungle-cat with those green eyes,' he said. 'I know who you are, without a doubt, but what about you? Do you need any form of identification before I get into your car?'

'I've seen your photograph,' she told him. ' I know who you are—unless you happen to have a double.'

'No double,' he answered, smiling. 'Let me have your keys, Kristen. I'll put the rest of my stuff in the boot.' He reached through the open window, unlocked the door and tossed his flight bag on to the back seat.

When they were on the way his watchfulness was something she sensed at once. She was also disturbingly aware of the attractive male scent of him, of his strange—and yet not so strange—nearness . . . and the stepped-up beating of her heart.

'By the way,' she said, 'Holly—she asked me to call her Holly, by the way—was upset during dinner. She thought you'd forgotten your promise. If you wake her, I'm not sure whether you'll be in for a wild reception—that is, until she cools off.'

'Cools of?' He laughed lightly. 'That's a polite way of putting it, Kristen.'

'No, really ... she's in one of her "anti" moods tonight. Well, she *was* until she went to bed.' Some of the anger she was feeling towards Ferdi began to wash off on him. 'I mean,' she lifted both hands from the wheel and then allowed them to drop back on to it, 'you certainly left things right to the very last minute, didn't you? She was so fed up that she said she'd prepare dinner for Christmas Eve and then have a kind of buffet lunch on Christmas Day.'

'I'm back, aren't I?' he said shortly. 'I caught the first available flight out and it's just one of those unfortunate problems that cropped up in Harare— some electrical fault.'

In the semi-darkness, beside her, she could feel his eyes going over her and she wished, suddenly, that she had changed into slacks and a top before leaving the flat, instead of turning up at the airport in the skimpy black top and flouncy black skirt she had worn to dinner to please Holly. One black, high-heeled sandal slipped on the clutch as she was changing gear and the car jibbed, and without stopping to think, she swore softly beneath her breath.

Beside her, Nick Lathbury said, 'Tut, tut.'

Ignoring him, she rolled down her window, but a spray of rain on her face caused her to roll it up again. She suddenly felt quite suffocated as she shared her car with this devastatingly handsome stranger who, thanks to Holly's many confidences, was not so much a stranger at all. Her thoughts flew to Barbro, the girl he was engaged to, and she felt a ridiculous tinge of pure jealousy.

'You'll have to direct me to your house,' she said abruptly. 'I don't know where it is.'

'I'll spend the night at Holly's,' he replied easily. 'After all, my car is there.'

He excited her and she resented this, so she shrugged. 'Just as you like.'

They were silent for a while and then he said again, 'Who's driving my aunt to drink? You?' He turned to look at her.

'No. As I said on the phone, I should imagine *you* are responsible for that.' There was a trace of anger in her voice, but the anger was really being aimed at Ferdi who, unlike Nick Lathbury, had not bothered to get back before Christmas Day. Visions of Ferdi flitted across her mind's eye and the fury she felt towards him at that moment was something like being dashed against jagged rocks, tearing at her, and she wanted to vent her feelings on the next best person— that person just happened to be Nick.

The orange-gold lights of street lamps filtered through the rain-streaked windows to fall, glittering, on her diamond engagement ring on one hand and to cause the ring of pearls and garnets, which Holly had insisted that she accepted on the occasion of her birthday, to glow on the ring-finger of her other hand. The gift had caused considerable ill-feeling, for Kristen had not wanted to accept what was, quite obviously, an expensive antique ring. Holly had become very hurt and had actually cried. Between sniffs, she had said, 'You're such a blessing, Kristen. I *adore* having you in the flat. Please take it, with all my love.'

Uncannily, Nick broke into these thoughts. 'By the way,' he said, 'I'm fascinated by your ring.'

Yes—*but which ring?* she thought a little wildly. How would he react to the fact that the expensive ring of pearls and garnets had come from his aunt?

'Thank you,' she murmured, purposely lifting her left hand from the steering wheel. 'I'm engaged. Holly has probably mentioned that in her letters.' She laughed lightly. 'She seems to have mentioned everything else.'

'The engagement ring is beautiful, naturally, but I was referring to the other ring, as it happens,' he said, and her heart skipped a beat. 'It's an heirloom, of course? It was quite the fashion, years ago, to wear pearls and garnets. There's a ring very much like it amongst the Lathbury trinkets.' He spoke carelessly enough, but Kristen's mind wailed—oh, no . . . for she had believed the ring had been purchased from a little 'bygones' shop, owned by a friend of Holly's. For some unexplained reason she could not bring herself to tell him that Holly had given her the ring, so she kept quiet.

'You're engaged,' Nick went on, 'to a guy named Ferdi, and yet here you are, alone but nevertheless looking sleekly fashionable and very beautiful, on Christmas Eve?' She knew he was leading her on.

After a moment she said stiffly, 'Ferdi is on a skiing holiday in the Alpine resort, Gstaad. He—hasn't been able to make it back for Christmas. I'm wearing *this*,' she looked down at her skirt, 'because I'd been dining with Holly. Just to let you know my side of the story . . . I'd been sharing a flat with my brother Craig— well, Holly sent you the cutting of the wedding. He was promoted to Cape Town soon afterwards. I had

every intention of staying on in the flat by myself . . .
but—out of the blue—the building was sold and all the
tenants including myself, were informed that unless
they wished to buy the flats they were renting, they
would have to find other accommodation. I didn't
want to buy a flat at such a ridiculous price, naturally.
We—that is Craig, Libby and myself—had become
quite friendly with Holly by this time, and Holly
offered me Em's flat.'

'Holly wrote, telling me about it,' Nick answered.
'Apparently she was delighted to allow Craig and
Libby the use of the Morris on the great day, and she
was very excited at forming a good friendship with
"young people".'

They turned into the drive of the Lathbury
mansion—the house, old, gracious and silent, glistened
in the rain and the striped pinky-beige and chocolate
sun-awnings over the two upstairs windows in the
centre of a big white gable dripped water on to the
pergola, beneath which stretched the full length of the
veranda below. At one end of the roof, the look-out
appeared mysterious.

Kristen parked the car to one side of the house and
turned to reach for her raincoat.

'Allow me,' said Nick, 'my arm just happens to be
longer than yours.'

She was aware of a light prickle of excitement as he
retrieved her coat from the back of the car and draped
it about her shoulders. She thought she could smell
Rochas cologne, but whatever it was, it added to the
excitement.

'You go on ahead,' he told her. 'I'll lock the car.'

'We'll have to go via my flat,' she said. 'I don't have
Holly's key, but in case of an emergency and at night

when we visit each other, we use the door in the corridor—just off my hallway.'

'And this is an emergency?' Beside her, he laughed softly as he loosened his tie and the top two buttons of his shirt.

'I'm not sure.' She tried to match his tone. 'I'll have to think about it. I'm going to check to see if Holly has a bed made up in the guest suite. If not, I'll have to make your bed.'

Undoing another button, he said, 'Although it's raining it's hot enough to sleep on top of the bed. It had started to snow, where I've just come from.'

Kristen felt jangled and tense as she watched him getting out of the car and, before she could open the door, he was at her side to help her out. Stepping out into the rain, she stood uncertainly next to sweet-smelling petunias which were growing in tubs next to the carport.

As she ran on long slender legs in the direction of the door to her flat, she knew Nick was watching her. She unlocked the door and went straight to the bathroom where she removed her wet coat and draped it over the side of the bath, then she made her way into Holly's part of the house.

Except for any foodstuff, which she had taken to the kitchen and put into the refrigerator, earlier on, the dining-room held all the sad, lonely evidence of two women having dined together on Christmas Eve. The maid was off duty but had come to an arrangement with Holly that she would come in first thing in the morning to clear and wash up before going off duty again. Although the room was full of antiques, Persian rugs, paintings and willow pattern plates, these things did nothing to lighten the sombreness of the space.

On her way through the drawing-room to the guest suite, Kristen stopped to turn on the coloured lights of the tall Christmas tree with its glittering tinsel, brilliant satin-sheened balls and white-lacquered, gold-glittered cones which surrounded the big red drum in which the tree stood.

The guest suite, Holly had told her, had belonged to Nick before he left home. There were two beds in the room and both were made up, and Kristen breathed a sigh of relief, then, with a quick look at the bathroom to check on towels and soap, hurried back to her own flat.

Nick Lathbury had just entered the flat and his dark hair glinted with rain. 'I've left the rest of my stuff in the car,' he told her. 'I'll collect it in the morning. I've got everything I need here, including a couple of bottles of Scotch from Duty Free.' He smiled and her eyes rested, fascinated, on the groove in one cheek. 'After all I've been through to get here, I could do with a Scotch, believe me,' he said. 'It was good to hear those wheels clunk into place, as we prepared to land, I can tell you.'

'You say—after all you've *been through*. Does that include my driving?' she asked, laughing a little.

'Did *I* say that?' He gave her a lazy, sexy smile.

A moment later she watched him as he glanced around the room. 'Nice work,' he commented. 'Quite a difference from when Em had it.' He came towards her and gave her the keys to her car, and she was aware of how tall—but not too tall—he was and how wide-shouldered—but not too wide-shouldered. He was, she thought, graceful in a completely masculine way. Nick met her eyes, suddenly, catching her unawares, and she felt her cheeks begin to flush.

'This must be the work of an interior designer,' he

was saying, while she tried to collect her wits.

'N-no—of course not. Everything I possessed fitted in very well.' Her eyes scanned the room and came to rest on Holly's yellow-wood chest of drawers which accommodated the ivory and gold telephone and a copper jug of ink-blue hydrangeas, then they went to the yellow-wood side-table, on which stood a beautiful lamp. 'Ah . . . the yellow-wood pieces belong to Holly, of course. By the way, I checked. Your bed *is* made up. What's more, there's even a bowl of yellow roses on the bedside table.'

'Well, Holly wasn't a Girl Guide for nothing and her motto to this day is "Be Prepared".' Once again, his deep blue eyes came to rest on her face and she felt her heart turn over.

'Come through and we'll have a drink first, then we'll wake Holly.' He glanced at his watch. 'It's going on for midnight. I'd like to make a phone call first, though.'

The phone call would be to Barbro, Kristen thought, feeling an insane stab of jealousy. She found herself thinking—well, why not have a drink with him? After all, where is Ferdi?

'I'll come in a moment or two,' she said.

'I've got the message. That means you're not coming.'

'No, I'll come. I want to towel my hair first. It's damp from the rain.'

After he had gone Kristen went through to her bedroom and studied her face in the mirror, then, after a few deft touches with make-up, she went through to the corridor and opened the door. He has good eyebrows, she was thinking. He wears his clothes well and his chin is firm—and he has a nice voice too.

The tree glistened and glittered in its corner, at the far end of the drawing-room—a room of such grand proportions that it took the breath away and which was filled mainly with French and English antiques. Persian rugs glowed red, emerald-green, gold and blue and large mirrors, in ornate gilt frames, reflected the gracious elegance of the past. The scent of roses, in silver bowls, was heavy.

Nick, she saw, was already on the phone which stood on an intricately carved table in the adjoining library which was separated from the drawing-room by means of a huge square arch.

With bated breath, she found herself listening as he asked to speak to Barbro and then, from where she was standing, she could see his frown as he said, 'Thank you. Do you know when she'll be back? No, that's quite okay. Just tell her Nick called.'

Kristen watched him as he came back into the drawing-room. 'I'll get some ice,' he was saying, 'and I'll be with you in a moment.'

Feeling suddenly disorientated, she said, 'No, I'll get it. While I'm getting it you can pour me a Martini, if you like.'

There was a vitality and a very special kind of magnetism about him, she thought on her way to the kitchen, and somehow he had managed to keep his tan alive—probably by using a lamp at a gymnasium in England. As he had put the phone down, though, his blue eyes had had an angry glitter.

He was at the Louis Quatorze antique table, which held an array of crystal decanters with gleaming silver labels hanging from each neck, when she came through with the ice.

Without looking up, he began to pour, and her eyes

went over his clothes, which were expertly tailored, and then went to his dark hair, which was styled and arranged to suit the lifestyle of a successful young executive. Although he was still wearing his jacket, his shirt was undone and he had flung his tie over the back of a chair. He turned and holding a glass in each hand, came towards her. As she waited for him, she began to turn the ring of pearls and garnets with her thumb.

As she took the glass from him she said, 'Holly's going to be thrilled when she discovers you've made it. She was beginning to give up.'

'I had every intention of getting back,' he said curtly, and she knew he was thinking of Barbro.

They both turned sharply as Holly came into the room.

'Kristen?' she was saying. 'My mouth is so dry, dear——' There was a gasp and then she exclaimed, 'Nick!' When did you get back?' She went on looking at him with sleep-drugged eyes.

Wrapped in a black cotton kimono, Holly watched Nick as he put his glass down, then went over to her and placing his hands on her shoulders he bent his head to kiss her. Kristen stood listening to him as he explained why his plane had been delayed and how, after he had phoned the house, she had picked him up at the airport.

When he had finished Holly said, 'I'm so thrilled to have Kristen living in the flat. She's an absolute angel, by the way—always going out of her way to be nice to me in one way or another.'

To change the subject Kristen said quickly, 'Holly, would you like me to make you a pot of tea?'

'No, thank you, dear. I'll tell you what I'd really

like, though, and that's a ginger-beer.' Holly patted her chest. 'I have acute indigestion. I should never have gone to bed on top of that huge meal.' Looking at Nick she said, 'Kristen and I have developed a wonderful friendship, and this friendship is based on a shared sensitivity.'

As she prepared a tray in the kitchen, Kristen felt Holly was overstepping the mark and she could feel the tension building up at the back of her neck.

Nick was telling his aunt a little about his extended business trip when she got back with the ginger-beer and at the same time, he was pouring himself another Scotch. Obviously, the fact that Barbro was not at home had angered him.

'Thank you, dear,' said Holly, accepting the drink. 'I'm looking forward to this, and you were right, I *did* have just a little too much to drink. We must show Nick your flat in the morning.' Turning to Nick she said, 'You'll be amazed at the transformation. Em had that flat looking so dull and we decided on a complete new colour-scheme for Kristen.'

'I came through Kristen's flat, actually,' said Nick. 'It's very attractive—what I saw of it.'

'Did you notice how well the yellow-wood pieces go with Kristen's own furniture? They give a delightful cottagey look to the flat, I think. We had a lot of fun working out where to put them. Kristen includes me in everything—it's such a treat.'

Feeling decidedly niggled now, Kristen found herself thinking she'd had very little option really, as Holly had virtually forced the yellow-wood furniture on her—not that it didn't look lovely . . .

'I was only there for five minutes,' Nick said.

In an effort to hide her embarrassment, Kristen

lifted her glass to her lips and took a sip of her drink and then said, 'You've been far too generous—all those plants and everything.'

'Good heavens, the plants were all there in the garden, child,' Holly answered. 'They just had to be dug up and potted into pretty urns, and I already had those.'

Kristen was aware of the subtle but unmistakable way in which Holly was going out of her way to show Nick how well they were getting on, whereas such a relationship with Barbro was impossible.

Nick went on rattling the ice-cubes in his glass. 'So you've both had a lot of fun?' He lifted his lashes to look at his aunt.

'We have, yes,' Holly answered. 'Although Kristen's a very busy girl she always has time for me. Craig and Libby are also charming. They were delighted to have the use of the Morris, by the way. As Craig put it—a dream come true for them. Soon after the wedding, Kristen moved in and there was more excitement as we got to work on her flat.'

Turning to Kristen, Nick asked, 'What kind of work do you do?'

'I'm a representative for House of Marini—a cosmetic firm,' she replied, and then took a deep breath and hoped she wouldn't faint from all the tension. 'My work involves quite a lot of travel, actually. I'm often away, although I have an office in town. You see, I'm on the road a lot—promoting and selling cosmetics.'

'Well, yes, I can see you must be a very busy person,' he answered. 'Not much time for relaxation, I should imagine.' His smile was brief.

'Kristen finds her new flat relaxing,' Holly said,

'don't you, dear? Especially the little patio off her dining-room. Em had that patio looking so dowdy with two brown benches. I could never understand how she could live with them. It looks quite different now, though. I got Micky to paint some cast-iron furniture and moved it all to the patio, along with more urns containing lovely big-leafed plants. Kristen eats out there a lot.'

Kristen's eyes were moody as she watched Nick's fingers move over his jaw, then he said, 'By the way, has Barbro phoned?' He glanced at Holly and their eyes held.

'She phoned a couple of days ago, asking whether I'd heard when you were coming back, and I hadn't, of course. Since then I haven't heard from her, but she took a lot of trouble designing and creating, if you can call it that, a Christmas card for me.'

'That was nice of her,' Nick replied.

'There was nothing nice about it at all. As usual, Nick, that girl went out of her way to upset me.' Holly was becoming incensed with the desire to complain about Barbro. 'A clear illustration is that Christmas card!'

'*That girl* just happens to be the girl I'm engaged to,' Nick answered curtly, and touching Holly on a sensitive point.

'And all the more's the pity,' she answered, while a helpless frustration surged through Kristen as she listened to her.

'I don't want to quarrel,' said Nick. 'I didn't come home in time for Christmas, just to quarrel.' He got up and went over to Holly and patted her shoulder. 'Come on . . .' He laughed lightly, but his blue eyes were furious. 'What is it with you?'

Holly shook herself free of him. 'Is that all you're going to say? There's a lot you're quite blind to, Nick, believe me. I'm not to blame all the time for the feeling which exists—but you'll just have to find her out for yourself. I'm not the difficult customer you believe me to be. Kristen's proof of this. I get on very well with Kristen. She fills my life with joy. I feel almost young again—*wanted*—and I'm not getting at you here, by the way. I'm getting at Barbro, because she has never made me feel this way, and what's more, she never will. Another thing, Kristen loves this old house—and everything in it. She's sensitive to these things, and I can't tell you what that means to me.'

There were tense undercurrents in the room now and Kristen felt rooted to the spot. Somewhere in the house a clock was chiming twelve, and Nick glanced at his watch. 'Happy Christmas,' he said, and kissed Holly on the cheek. 'Come on, let's forget this nonsense.'

Trying desperately to hide her feelings, Kristen kissed Holly and then Nick kissed her, and his face smelled of expensive soap and shaving lotion. When the kiss was over Kristen adjusted one strap of the black top she was wearing and her hand was shaking. She saw Nick's dark blue eyes go to the ring of pearls and garnets and, although he was still smiling, his eyes were speculative and, in view of the strange elements running through Holly's conversation during the course of the last half hour or so, she dropped her hand quickly. Something told her he had decided that the ring was, in fact, one of the Lathbury 'trinkets', and she felt the promise of trouble to come.

'I must go,' she said, anger beginning to burn within her.

'Allow me to see you back to your flat,' Nick said.

'For goodness' sake, I only have to go through the door in the corridor!' For Holly's benefit, Kristen tried to smile.

'Nevertheless I am, I hope, the perfect gentleman. I'll see you to the door. After all, this is a big house.' His smile did not disguise the fact that, since she had met him at the airport, his mood had altered.

At the door in the corridor he said, 'So you've quite settled in?' He spoke pleasantly enough. 'And obviously you get along with Holly.'

'She's a wonderful person.' Kristen found herself stammering. 'She's so kind it's——'

'Well, yes,' he cut in, still in that same easy voice, 'she's kind—and generous. I guess it's easy to like someone like that.' For a moment, his eyes locked with hers. 'I imagine I can speak frankly, Kristen. Be careful not to encourage the antagonism which exists between Holly and my fiancée—no matter how innocently.'

Before Kristen could think of a thing to say he turned and left her, and she felt the sudden fury leap up—right into her eyes.

CHAPTER TWO

STRETCHING, cat-like, Kristen turned in her bed and began to measure her loneliness on Christmas morning. Her thoughts then went to the night before and to Nick Lathbury's insulting remark as he had said good night to her—the message in his dark blue eyes there to confirm his sudden disapproval of her. Holly's foolish remarks had been intended to sting Nick, and they had.

According to the view through the windows, it was a glorious day with a blue sky, brilliant sunshine, and the air that drifted into the room was scented. There was no sign of the rain which had fallen the night before.

Kristen had been in a lonely, depressed mood during the past two months and it frightened her, because it was an aimless, unhappy and brooding frame of mind and a period during which she had asked herself a lot of hopeless questions—all revolving around Ferdi Jaeger. On a sudden impulse, Ferdi had decided to go on a skiing holiday and he had chosen Gstaad where, he had said casually enough, there were good hotels and lively nightlife. He had gone away, leaving her utterly depressed, using the money he had saved towards their honeymoon, and although he had promised to be back in time for Christmas, he was still away. Except for a postcard of brightly-clad people preparing to ski down snow-glittered slopes, he had not even bothered to write during the past month. On the card he had written—'Having a fabulous time. No bones broken, thanks to a super instructress. Ferdi.' Just Ferdi!

Unable to cope with her thoughts another moment, Kristen sat up and, drawing her knees up to her chin, brushed her dark red hair back from her face with her hands. Certainly today she did not feel glamorous, sophisticated and successful—which was Holly's description of her. Brooding was inevitable, she thought, and seemed likely to continue right through the day, and she would ask herself whether she was still in love with Ferdi . . . It was a question she had been asking herself before he went away, actually, but she had refused to face up to it.

She had just finished her breakfast and was considering getting dressed for church when there was a knock on the panelled door to her entrance hall and, still wearing a short nightdress, she hurried to her bedroom for a robe which she put on and wrapped about her slender body. She was still tying the belt when she opened the door, and she tensed as she saw Nick Lathbury standing there. Holly's Siamese cat, Nefertiti, had followed him and was rubbing her smoky black-marked body against his long legs and looking up at him with eyes of blue. Her mews were demanding, as only those of a Siamese cat can be.

Nick, Kristen thought a little wildly, seemed to have been created to wear jeans and a denim shirt, and his looks were quite stunning. His eyes reminded her of deep blue lochs and she had the feeling that women could disappear into them and never be seen again.

After a moment he said, 'You look very provocative, wrapped as you are in honey-coloured satin.'

In view of the fact that he had offended her the

night before she said, 'Well, if I do it's certainly not the result of careful planning on my part, if that's what you're suggesting.' Suddenly, she found herself hating him for the emotions he stirred in her—which were incongruous and absurd. 'It's certainly not my intention to look—or try to look—provocative. Let's just say that I'm still in my nightdress because it is, after all, Christmas morning and, into the bargain, very early. I wasn't prepared for visitors.'

'I see you're as full of spirit as you're beautiful,' he observed.

'Why don't you just add "and as cunning" and be done with it?' she snapped. 'Because that's what you mean, isn't it?'

He went on looking at her and then he said, 'Let's face it, Kristen, you're hostile—but then intruders can be a disruptive force, and I guess I am just that.'

'That's not what I said, is it? I happened to say I wasn't prepared for visitors. I have no reason to look on you as an intruder in my life. The word intruder has a menacing ring to it. What you really mean, Nicholas, is that you believe yourself to be an intruder and a disruptive force in my happy relationship with your aunt.' Gold flecks danced in her eyes. 'Anyway, I take it you've come for the car keys. I'll go and get them. Just a moment.' She turned away, feeling ruffled and at a disadvantage in her satin robe, and she knew that he was following her with his eyes as he stood in the small paved and walled-in area next to the door which had a coral and white striped sun-canopy over it and an area where earthenware pots (Holly's again and at her insistence) spilled petunias of mauve, deep purple and pink. Nearby, in another great earthenware pot, a lemon tree was strung with small fruit which were on their way to becoming larger and turning yellow.

When she came back from her bedroom she found that Nick had invited himself into her sitting-room. Early-morning light sparkled everywhere, and when he looked at her his eyes seemed to gather more intense blue and she felt her senses beginning to swim.

The room was as lovely in the morning as it was at night when light came from beautiful lamps. The one single diamond on Kristen's finger sparkled—a taunting reminder of Ferdi, while on her other hand, Holly's circle of pearls and garnets gathered burgundy lights which became reflected in the pearls.

'When you've finished with the keys, please leave them next to the telephone,' she instructed, 'and now, if you'll excuse me, I have things to do.'

'Kristen,' he said, 'about last night——'

'I don't wish to talk about last night,' she cut in swiftly. She turned away from him—then caught her breath as he reached for her wrist and pulled her round to face him.

'I was being frank last night, and I think you know why. Holly and Barbro don't get on and you must seem like a gift from heaven to Holly right now. Be kind to Holly by all means. Be sympathetic—but don't overdo it, right?'

'I'll do as I damn well like!' she snapped, snatching her wrist away. 'My good terms with your aunt have nothing to do with you—or Barbro. I have no wish to discuss this.' Turning her back on him again, she went through to her bedroom, where she knew he could hardly follow her and where she stood shaking with nerves and anger.

When she went back into the sitting-room, some

time later, the keys were on the yellow-wood chest-of-drawers and, for a long moment, her moody eyes rested on them. Thinking about everything, she felt insulted by Nicholas Lathbury, crushed by Ferdi and let-down and smothered by Holly. The apprehension she had been feeling lately about renting this lovely flat from this over-generous woman was beginning to turn to anger. How dared Holly use her to fuel the feud which involved Barbro? In this uncharitable mood, she thought, how could she go to church?

She went on fuming as she showered, although she tried not to think about a thing, and then going back to her bedroom she got dressed and was wearing white cotton trousers and a top which was a reckless riot of blue, jade-green and fuchsia-pink but which had narrow black shoulder straps, when Holly knocked at her door.

'I've come to wish you a Happy Christmas again, dear, and to thank you once more for going to the airport for Nick last night. How sweet of you!'

Looking at her, Kristen felt suddenly tried, but she smiled and said, 'Fortunately, I heard the phone. I didn't want to disturb you, so I arranged with—er—Nick to pick him up at the airport. He was going to phone an all-night taxi rank in Durban. It must have been a wonderful surprise to find that he *had* got back in time for Christmas, after all.' It was just as well, she thought, that Holly did not know what was going on in her mind right now.

'Oh, it was. Usually Nick is very dependable,' Holly answered. She was wearing a deep purple sun-frock, which hung in a straight line from the shoulder straps. It was a dress suited to a much younger women, but in view of the fact that Holly was slim and her silver hair was arranged sleekly back from a beautifully chiselled face, she was able to wear the dress and appear quite stunning. An antique Egyptian pendant of silver with a deep purple gemstone embedded in an intricate setting emphasised her elegant if slightly eccentric brand of elderly beauty.

'I'll let you into a little secret, Kristen,' she was saying, 'Barbro wasn't at home when Nick phoned again this morning. Oh, he's trying to appear very nonchalant about it, but I can see he's absolutely furious. Instead of keeping to my plans about following last night's Christmas Eve dinner with a cold buffet at lunch today, I decided to cook another big dinner today, but Nick says he refuses to have me cooking all morning and he wants to take you and me out to Christmas lunch at the Edward Hotel.'

Thinking of the undercurrents of the night before, Kristen said quickly, 'Oh, Holly ... how very kind, and thank you—and Nick—so much, but—er— something has cropped up, and now that Nick is home, I—er—partly accepted. I was coming to ask you whether you'd mind if I didn't have Christmas luncheon with you—well now, of course, dinner at the Edward, as it happens.' She closed her eyes briefly and felt sick at making up the useless story. 'You see,' she went on, 'I've been invited out—oh, it's a long story really, and I won't go on about it but I do hope you'll understand?'

Holly's face changed very slightly, but when she answered, she sounded pleasant enough. 'Not at all, dear, if that's what you'd like. By the way, I was very naughty last night ... I went to bed and forgot to give you your little present. I loved that beautiful book— *Country Houses and Gardens*. Thank you so much.'

The 'little present' turned out to be a Flokati rug, made from pure New Zealand wool and which Holly had placed next to a flowering shrub, to one side of the door. 'It's for your study,' she added. 'I know it's what you had in mind.'

'Oh, Holly!' There was dismay in Kristen's voice. 'What am I to do with you? You're far too generous ...' Her voice trailed away and she felt trapped. How was she to cope with Holly's overwhelming generosity? 'It's beautiful. Thank you so much, but I—it's just beyond me ... I mean—a Flokati rug!'

'I got a lot of pleasure choosing this for you,' Holly answered, 'and a whole lot more giving it to you. I hope you have a lovely time today. I don't know how I'm going to face another enormous dinner.' She patted her flat stomach. 'I already feel like an old ship which has been loaded to its Plimsoll line, but I'm going to enjoy myself, anyway.'

Kristen laughed politely, but she was utterly depressed. 'You'll never resemble an old ship which has been loaded to its Plimsoll line, Holly, and that's the main thing. I wish *I* had your flat tummy.'

'My dear, *you* have the body of a goddess!' Holly answered. 'You're a very beautiful and charming young girl.'

Some time later, and feeling the comforting glow of the sun, Kristen walked to her car and then opened the door and slid behind the steering wheel, but then, on second thoughts, she got out and went round to the boot and opened it. Nick had taken all his belongings.

When he spoke she turned quickly, and in doing so, she stumbled on the crazy-paving and Nick steadied her with both hands. 'So you've decided to forsake us.'

'Yes.' Her voice was cool. Looking into those deep blue eyes, she experienced that odd sense of danger again.

'There was no need to change your plans,' he went on. 'I know you'd planned to spend Christmas Day with Holly.' He went on looking at her.

'Things have changed now,' she replied. 'You're home on Christmas Day and under the circumstances I feel—free to go my own way.' Feeling the power of his eyes, she wondered whether he had guessed that there was absolutely no truth in her story. She went on, 'I thought you and Holly and Barbro would like to be together. This is, after all, a family time.' She shook her hair back from her face and glanced away.

He laughed at this, then he said, 'Don't tell me that Holly hasn't put you wise to the fact that Barbro will not be having dinner with us.'

'In any case—I prefer to be with friends.' She did not look at him.

'Fine.' He stepped back. 'Have a pleasant day.'

'As they say in the supermarkets,' she said, turning to look at him, 'and might I wish you the same?— Have a pleasant day, Nicholas.' There was a touch of anger in her voice.

Now that she had committed herself by pretending that she was going to be with friends, she realised that she had no option but to drive somewhere. The drive to the Valley of a Thousand Hills proved to be frustrating, so she turned the car and headed back to Durban's beach-front.

After parking the car on the Lower Marine Parade she sat staring at the sea and brooding about Ferdi in between trying to shove Nick Lathbury out of her restless mind.

In his last letter, received well over a month ago, Ferdi had very casually referred to a girl who had taught him a lot about skiing. This, then, was the instructress. Her name was Reba. The name revolved round and round in her mind.

'Why don't you think of something else,' she whispered fiercely, 'somebody else. Like Vasco de Gama, maybe.' Strangely enough, she recalled long-ago history lessons—Vasco de Gama, the Portuguese navigator, had sighted land when making his way to the East on Christmas Day towards the end of 1497, and he had called it Natal. Her eyes scanned the beach and then went to the sea again. Had he been as lonely as she was right now? she wondered.

Suddenly she was furious. Why should she be sitting here when she had a perfectly lovely flat in which to spend Christmas Day? Purposely, she had refused any invitations which had come her way for the simple reason that she did not want to feel that she was in the way. She should, she thought, have boarded a plane and visited Craig and Libby—after all, they had asked her to do this—instead of being landed in an impossible situation where she felt she had to get away from Holly and her aggravatingly handsome nephew.

Her mind continued to flit about restlessly, brooding on one subject and then another. Time dragged on and she concentrated on the gulls as they flew overhead and the holidaymakers on the beach—the people who would be having Christmas dinner at night at the exciting variety of plush hotels on the Upper Marine Parade ... hotels which were large enough to cater for casual guests who wished to eat dinner at one or for those who preferred a grand dinner at night.

It was late enough, she knew, to be thinking about going home, but she continued to sit and brood, and when a car swung into the parking space next to her own, she turned away irritably so that she was sitting sideways in her seat.

After a moment, she heard a door slam and then Nick Lathbury said, 'You've been sitting here a long time.' He had come to the passenger side of her car and was looking at her through the open window. Before she could gather her wits about her, he had come round to her side and she felt like sinking through the floor of the Mazda.

'What makes you think I've been sitting here a long time?' she asked.

'I don't have to remind you, do I, that the Edward Hotel is just up there? I had lunch with Holly, but we drove down here first and I spotted your car. After lunch I came back so that Holly could see the waves again and you were still here. I took Holly home, since she wanted a nap, and the desire to see whether you were still here overcame me.' He spoke on a note of mockery that angered her.

'It seems to amuse you, to see me sitting here,' Kristen retorted.

'Why *are* you sitting here?' he asked. When she made no reply he said, 'I was worried about you.'

'That's—that was very thoughtful of you.' Her voice was stiff with sarcasm. She turned away from him and her eyes went to the sleek, dark green Jaguar which was parked next to her Mazda. Looking at him again, she said, 'Did Holly see me sitting here?' Her voice was accusing.

'No, she didn't. You didn't have a lunch date, did you?'

'I changed my mind.' Unable to meet his gaze, she fussed with her engagement ring, turning it round and round.

'You don't really expect me to believe that?' he asked in a more friendly tone. 'Something's bothering you, right?'

She watched him as he turned away and then came back to the passenger side of the car, and after opening the door, he got in beside her.

On an impulse she said, 'I'm worried and depressed, if you must know.'

'That's no reason to starve yourself, surely?'

'I haven't heard from Ferdi for well over a month,' she found herself saying.

'Perhaps you have a rival.' Kristen saw his eyes go to the engagement ring on her finger.

In a furious voice she demanded, 'How do you feel, after having said that? Does it make you feel good?'

'Nothing makes me feel good right now,' he answered. 'Anyway, you might have to give that lovely big diamond back.'

She was, somehow, aware of the challenge. He knows about the ring, she thought. He knows it's *the ring*. During the meal at the Edward, Holly must have told him. By this time, Nick knew just why his eyes had been drawn to it on the way from the airport. The ring had seemed familiar to him in a vague way . . .

'In case you don't know,' she said, 'Holly gave me the garnet and pearl ring for my birthday.'

'I *do* know,' he said, without any change in his expression.

Kristen was thinking a little wildly that Holly would have told Nick anything to show how much she adored the girl who was renting her flat, whereas any sort of relationship with the girl he was engaged to was out of the question.

Glancing down at the ring, she said, 'I know it's a good ring, and I didn't want to accept it. I was—overwhelmed, actually.'

She turned to look at him and saw that his gaze was scanning the beach and the sea beyond. 'The ring is no big deal,' he said, but the mildness of his tone was belied by the sudden hard look in his blue eyes.

'But—obviously—you ...' Kristen found herself stammering. 'Obviously, this ring means something to you. I mean,' she lifted her shoulders, 'you remarked on my wearing it on the way from the airport. I realised, from the moment I saw it, that it could have been an heirloom, but I imagined Holly had bought it from her friend—the friend who owns a bygones shop.' While she was speaking she felt a wild rush of anger towards Holly for having given the ring to her. 'I'll give it back,' she said.

Nick swung round to look at her. 'Forget about it. What Holly does with her possessions has nothing to do with me, Kristen. You're welcome to it.'

'It sounds like it!' She looked at him with angry eyes. 'You say forget it and yet you recognised the ring in the car—*at night*! That's how interested you really are.' Suddenly the ocean's thunder sounded very loud.

'You may find it hard to believe this—but I didn't recognise the ring on the way from the airport, although the setting seemed vaguely familiar. After all, why should I have thought Holly had given it to you? It was very fashionable to wear garnets and pearls, at one time. There are a lot of rings like this one, in family trinket boxes.'

'This is no *trinket*!' One tiny shoulder strap of the

floral top she was wearing had slipped down and she moved away quickly as he put one finger under it and slid it up into position. She struggled against the acceleration of her senses.

'What are you doing tonight?' he asked her.

'Since I'm without energy or inspiration—nothing,' she retorted.

'I'd like to change that. Come to a party with me.'

'Because you're at a loose end, is that it?' she asked sarcastically.

'Well, so are you, aren't you?'

With a spurt of anger she said, 'You'd get a shock if I said yes, wouldn't you?' She was thinking of Ferdi and feeling decidedly deflated.

'So in other words, you're saying yes?'

'I didn't say that. I'm saying no, actually.'

'Why say no when this character in Gstaad has let you down? What do you think *he's* doing right now? Dreaming of *you*?'

'You're absolutely insensitive,' she replied quickly.

'Don't disappoint me,' he said. 'I've already told them I'd be bringing you along.'

'So it's important to you that I go with you?' Her voice contained spite.

'Yes, as it happens.'

Kristen took a little breath and felt suddenly exhilarated about going out somewhere.

'What about Holly?' she asked.

'Holly is entertaining members of the Garden Club.'

On sheer impulse she said, 'I'll go.'

'Fine. I'm going back to my town house, but I'll pick you up at seven-thirty.' Tall and lean, Nick lifted his knees and, opening the door, shifted his feet from

the car to the ground and stood up, in one easy
movement. He stooped to look in at her. 'I'll be seeing
you.' Their eyes clung together before he straightened
and went back to his dark green Jaguar and starting it
immediately, reversed out from the parking bay and,
without giving her another look, drove off.

Kristen found herself depressed again—and yet
happy at the same time. Her fingers stroked the
wrist of one hand and she took a long breath. The
air was moist and there was a violet haze over the
horizon, and she began to think about going back to
her flat.

When Nick called for her at seven-thirty, his dark
blue eyes went over her, and without being vain she
knew she was looking sleek and rather beautiful in a
black, layered organdie dress which emphasised her
slenderness. Her auburn hair hung to her shoulders
and, although she was not particularly tall, she looked
long-legged and slim. As their eyes met she felt as if
Nick had actually touched her.

He was a good driver, she noticed at once, and
compared his driving with Ferdi's careless manner in
handling a car.

Nick took her to a house high on a hill on the North
Coast and where there was a glittering view of Durban
in the far distance as the coastline curved. It was a
house which seemed to have been designed with
entertaining in mind and it seemed to have everything
to offer in the line of indoor and outdoor relaxation.
Lights spilled from it to shimmer and jump on the
surface of a swimming pool and a sense of spatial flow
was aided by the use of white Italian tiles which
extended throughout the house and out to the patio,
beside the pool. Two soft-grey poodles, with brilliant

collars and manicured nails, clicked about the cool tiles.

Kristen's excited eyes went to the enormous white beams which stretched from the strip of wall above the sliding glass doors of the lounge and were supported by tubular pillars. These two pillars were embedded on either side of the pool and added more dramatic reflections to the water.

Jazz music came from the house and the piano often took command over sounds created by other instruments. At the particular moment, it was more piano and drums enjoying a sensual and tantalising game together. The music acted as an immediate tease to the senses and Kristen found herself thinking—to hell with Ferdi Jaeger in Gstaad!

She and Nick were greeted warmly enough by Frank and Donna Prentice, who owned the house, yet, whilst being handed drinks, Kristen was aware of a tension between Frank and Donna and she could only put this down to the fact that Nick was not with Barbro.

Frank was saying, rather stiffly, 'And how is Elizabeth, Nick?'

There was a small silence, then Nick said, 'Oh, on top form, as usual.' There was no expression on his face and then, looking at Kristen, he said, 'Frank is the only one who ever calls my eccentric aunt Elizabeth, by the way.'

'Oh . . .' She smiled politely, finding herself at a sudden disadvantage with the Prentices.

When she and Nick were alone she gazed around the room with its low straight-backed white sofas piled high with cushions which had picked up the pinks, gold, mauves and pale blues of the magnificent Dhurry rug on the white-tiled floor.

'Nick,' she said after a moment, 'who are these people?'

He ran his finger round the rim of his glass. 'Why do you ask?'

'Well . . . they're so very snobby.' She drew the words out. 'They appear to be so rich—and I don't feel very welcome.'

'They're rich,' he answered, 'but not excessively so. Snobby?' He hoisted one shoulder. 'Well, I don't know.' He gave her a mocking glance. 'Admittedly, the house is very, very impressive, but it happens to have been designed for a fun lifestyle.'

'Frank, if you'll pardon me for saying so, doesn't look like a fun person.' She laughed a little. 'What does he do?'

'Well, to some extent, he takes life seriously. You see, he makes his money by pleading for people in a court of law.'

'Oh . . . you mean he's an advocate?' Kristen took a sip of her drink and looked at him over the rim of her glass.

'Uh-huh.'

'Anyway, I don't think it was very wise of you to have asked them whether you could bring me along instead of Barbro, Nick. I'm feeling very uncomfortable. Obviously, the Prentices don't approve.'

'Let me get you another drink,' he suggested. As he took her glass from her she shook her head a little, as if to throw off confusion. 'When I come to think of it you've probably had nothing much to eat all day,' Nick said.

'Oh,' she laughed suddenly, 'I grabbed a bit of cheese from the refrigerator when I got back from the beach.'

'You still haven't told me if you're hungry,' he said. 'Would you like to eat now?'

'I don't mind eating later,' she told him. 'It's fun looking around.'

'Let me get you another drink, then.' He took her arm and she walked with him through to the lounge which was massed with flowers chosen to repeat the exact shades of the Dhurry rug and heaped cushions on the white sofas and chairs. A bar, which was all white and had blue and white mugs hanging from white rafters, was situated at the far end of the room.

Touching Nick, by accident, caused an unwelcome little thrill, and her eyes went to his well-shaped hands and long fingers. As she moved away from him quickly she found herself thinking that Nick Lathbury was bad news.

After her third and, for her, reckless drink she found herself relaxing, and in a blissful haze, she smiled at Nick as he offered her a blue and white bowl piled high with purple olives.

'Tell me when you'd like to dance,' he said, reaching for another blue and white bowl piled high with dusky, yellow-green olives this time, which made her giggle.

'Would you like to dance?' he asked again, and thinking about his thighs against her own she sobered. 'Not now.' She cradled her glass between slender fingers. 'I'm a sipper. I like to sip my drink.'

'Well, in that case, let's take our glasses outside. There's a glittering view of curved coastline and Durban from the garden,' he said.

They went outside and past the Italian-tiled patio where people were dancing. When they reached the lawn, Kristen could feel the dew through her sandals.

'Oh, how beautiful!' she exclaimed, when she saw the view. 'Don't the lights of Durban look sensational in the distance?' Far below them, directly in front, tier upon tier of breakers appeared luminous in the dark and further along the beach the sea thundered over the rocks and creamed over the tidal strip.

Nick was standing so close to her that their bodies were touching.

'What should we talk about?' he asked.

Feeling silly and suddenly very flighty, she said, 'I don't know. I'll have to think about it.'

Beside her, in the darkness, he lifted his glass to his lips.

After a moment she said, 'Nick, I wish I could understand you.' She could feel the warmth of him next to her and felt herself beginning to float hazily. She thought—I feel a little drunk and I think I'm falling in love with him.

'Why is it necessary for you to understand me?' His voice was soft, but the words carried force.

'That's intelligent, isn't it?' She turned to look at him. 'You're Holly's nephew, after all.'

'And that makes all the difference?' He made a gesture, still holding his glass in his hand.

'I think so—yes.'

'Well, for one thing, I don't like surprises,' he said.

'Oh, I see ... And finding me in Holly's flat came as a surprise? Perhaps you'd expected to find another Em? Someone nearer to your aunt's age?'

'Finding you there was no surprise,' he answered. 'I'd expected to find you there. After all, Holly had written, and she had also sent me a cutting from the newspaper which covered your brother's wedding.'

He reached for her glass and placed it with his own

on the low wall in front of them. Then he put his elbows on the parapet and, as he did so, his body touched hers again.

'What surprises me is that I want, very much, to make love to you,' he said and, for a moment, silence hung between them.

'You know,' she said, 'I can't think of a thing I might have done wrong. The way you say that makes it sound like an insult. I mean, apart from the fact that I accepted this ring—and I've said I'll give it back—I don't know what I've done to warrant all this. I'm just waiting for the right moment to return the ring. Holly can be very touchy.'

'I've told you to forget about the ring.' Nick spoke in a hard voice. 'The ring isn't going to make a big difference in my life.'

Suddenly he bent across her and his mouth found hers, and she was immediately invaded by a passionate desire to have his arms close about her. When he took his mouth away she said, 'You seem to forget the fact that you're engaged.'

'I haven't forgotten,' he told her. 'I just don't want to be reminded about it, that's all.'

As he took her into his arms she felt a rising panic which soon gave way to sensual pleasure. He stroked her back with his hands, drawing her closer, and she couldn't prevent herself from responding. Vaguely, Kristen knew she was on dangerous ground. After all, he was engaged to be married and so was she . . . but where were the two other characters involved?

Nick moved his thighs against her own and she felt herself go weak with longing. She found herself wondering whether his whole body was as tanned as his face and arms. The pressure of his mouth on hers increased and she had to stifle the urge to part her lips for him. When he parted her lips with his tongue the sensation was like an electrical shock to her. She had always kept her lips pressed firmly together when Ferdi had tried to do this to her.

There were sounds of people making their way to the Prentices' view site, and Nick released her suddenly.

'Great minds think alike,' he said. 'Come, I could use another drink and something to eat, and I'm sure that must go for you too. You must be starving.'

In a small, shaken voice she said, 'I'm ravenous.'

As soon as they entered the house, Frank Prentice came towards them and, gesturing towards a long buffet table, said, 'I haven't seen you two eating.' His eyes rested briefly on Kristen and she felt he was sizing her up and comparing her to the beautiful— from what she had heard—Barbro and wondering, no doubt, what the devil Nick was up to.

To hide her confusion she said, 'I think you have a tremendous house, by the way. It's very exciting.'

Frank's regard was cool and polite. 'I'm glad you like it. Nick will tell you I had a very good architect— not to mention an excellent designer, Barbro, so it's not surprising that the final result is effective.' Frank's smile was humourless.

Kristen felt a stab of jealousy which, in turn, gave way to anger. Why hadn't Nick told her this? After Frank had left them she considered Nick with cold, golden-green eyes.

'Why didn't you tell me?' she demanded. 'I made a complete fool of myself!'

'In what way?' he asked.

'Well . . . I might as well have brought Barbro right into this room.'

Nick made a gesture of anger with his shoulders. 'Come and have something to eat,' he said.

As she helped herself to pheasant Kristen said, 'I'm surprised Frank Prentice didn't ask to see my credentials when we arrived, and have done with it. I don't know whether to be on my guard or to overlook his churlishness towards me and just enjoy the party. I shouldn't have come, actually.' Looking across the room, she encountered Frank's grey, speculative gaze and was conscious of a sudden flare of antagonism in it.

'Relax.' Nick's voice was impatient. 'Let me remind you of something—even when people are engaged, they're separate personalities and entitled to break away now and then.'

'This is the first time I've—er—broken away, since my engagement,' she said, 'and, I'm already regretting it.'

'I don't think you should be telling me this,' he replied, with something like mockery in his voice.

'Why not?'

'Because I don't believe you *are* regretting it. You enjoyed being in the garden with me, didn't you?'

'I knew that had to come up!' Her voice was bitter. 'I've played right into your hands, haven't I?'

A number of people went out of their way to greet Nick, and while she ate her food Kristen watched on with moody eyes, then tensed when she heard one attractive girl say, 'I don't want to give you a hard time, Nick, but where's Barbro?'

'Oh,' Nick shrugged casually, 'something cropped up . . .'

As they walked to where Nick's Jaguar was parked, some time later, Kristen found herself saying, 'They probably think you're having a secret affair with me.'

'I can live with that,' he said. 'I won't have troubled sleep over it, that's for sure.' He stopped walking suddenly, and took her into his arms. 'So—what are we bickering about?'

As his mouth sought hers they could hear the strains of a piano medley, slow and tantalising, and she felt the night closing in about her and, exhilarated by what was, for her, too much to drink, she found herself straining towards him.

Nick's hand went to her breast and then, abruptly, he brought her to her senses by undoing her arms from his neck and holding her away from him.

'I'll be honest with you,' he said, 'I brought you here to suit my own purpose. In other words, I schemed to manipulate you into going to bed with me afterwards. I realise, suddenly, that this poses certain problems . . . I'll take you home now.'

When Kristen had managed to get herself together she said, 'I hope you're joking, Nick. If not, you've got a nerve! Make no mistake, I have no intention of allowing you to manipulate me into going to bed with you.'

After he had dropped her off she went inside and immediately ran a bath, then, sliding down in the water, she hid her body beneath foaming bathsalts.

CHAPTER THREE

KRISTEN had been sleeping on her stomach, the frilly pillowslip was covered with a mass of dark red hair. As she turned over, she lifted her arms and smoothed the silken strands back from her face. There was birdsong coming from the garden and her eyes lingered on the curtains which moved in the breeze and the sunlit patterns of light and shadow on the walls. Altogether, it was a very lovely and cheerful room to wake up in, she thought.

This morning she was anything but cheerful, however, and her thoughts went to the night before when Nick had, not very gently, taken her arms from his neck, shocking her and bringing her to her senses. If only Ferdi had kept his promise about coming back for Christmas, then none of this would have happened.

She took her breakfast out to the patio, which led off the dining-room with its coral-pink carpeting and delicate light gold dining-suite, which she had been fortunate enough to buy at a sale. Her thoughts brooded on Nick Lathbury who seemed, so suddenly, to resent everything about her—so much so that he had callously thought to manipulate her into going to bed with him.

Glancing round the walled-in paved area which had been made so much more picturesque by having Holly's heavy and intricately scrolled cast-iron furniture to grace it, Kristen felt a spurt of anger towards Holly for going out of her way to let Nick know how she had enjoyed having Micky Naidoo move the furniture to the patio. Although Holly had not meant it that way, it had shown her up in an unflattering manner to Nick. Alcoves set into white walls held potted plants and geraniums which were in full bloom and almost the same colour as the carpet in the dining-room. Holly had seen to that!

From where she was seated at the table which was covered with a floor-length cotton cloth the colour of pink roses, she could see the Indian Ocean in the distance.

Throughout the day there was no sign of Holly, which was unusual, she thought, until she remembered that Em's daughter had called for Holly in the morning and must have taken her to visit Em. Nick, she knew, had gone back to his house.

She felt restless and tried to overcome it by rearranging certain pieces of furniture and then by going through her wardrobe with a critical eye. Christmas, she thought dismally, had come to an end, and tomorrow she would be back at work which, apart from other duties, involved visiting pharmacies, beauty clinics and hair-stylist salons. It was interesting work, but there were times when she did not feel like driving from one town to another. Often, she had to book into a motel for a night, and the same thing might happen again, for she had a long journey to the North Coast ahead of her the next day.

She devoted the evening to doing her nails, and although she hoped not to spend the following night away from home, she packed an overnight bag—which was something she always did, anyway, because she never knew what the future held in store for her. There was always the possibility of car trouble, delays—or even bad storms which made driving hazardous, so she packed the usual items—a night-dress, a caftan, toothbrush, toothpaste, cosmetics, a fresh blouse, trousers, skirt and undies. Often, on her travels, she had been thankful she had gone prepared. In her present fluttery state of mind she couldn't make up her mind what soap to take, just in case she needed soap. Libby had sent, from Cape Town, two tablets of Puig luxury floral soap—mimosa and azalea rhodo-dendron, and becoming heartily sick of·her dithering and uncertainty, she almost threw the mimosa tablet into her travel bag. When she looked in a drawer for the key to Holly's beach house, Salt Air, which was situated at a small settlement called Surprise Bay, she could not find it and then thoroughly lost her temper when she eventually did find it—staring her in the face. The key to the beach house meant a lot to her, since she had often had to stay there overnight after coming to the conclusion that she would never make it back to Durban before midnight.

By eight the following morning, businesslike in a black linen suit and white frothy organdie blouse, she was on her way. Christmas was over, but Holly's tall Christmas tree, which almost touched the high ceiling of the formal drawing-room, would remain there in the traditional way until after the New Year.

Normally, when she had long distances to cover, Kristen preferred to wear well-tailored summer or winter trousers, with a matching jacket and the kind of blouse she was wearing now. Today, though, she had an important appointment at a plush new beauty salon at an equally brand new shopping mall just outside Durban on the North Coast, where she was to show a new range of make-up revolving around rouge, blush-creme, eye-shadow pencils, waterproof mascara and lip and nail gloss, so she had set out on her long journey wearing a suit. In her job, she had become a disciplined and polished young woman, in control of her life—or so she had thought, until Ferdi Jaeger and Nicholas Lathbury had come into it.

After her stop at the beauty salon she walked to her car and, before getting into it, removed her un-crushable linen jacket and tossed it into the back seat. It had, quite suddenly, become a hot, stifling day and there was a heavy, dark haze over the sea.

She knew she was running late and drove quickly and somewhat impatiently, her golden-green eyes concentrating on the road which was busy with heavy traffic on its way to the canefields and sugar estates. From time to time, views of the sea presented themselves through breaks in the hills, but although there were no clouds, the sea looked menacing and lacked glitter.

While Kristen ate a green salad lunch at a small motel she felt a rising panic when she saw just how late she was running, especially as the weather seemed to be changing all the time. Although, so far, her day had run smoothly, she still had a long way to cover and, with thoughts that Ferdi might telephone, she was desperate to get back home to her flat in Durban.

Her last stop was Richards Bay—a natural bay which had always been a favourite resort of fishermen and naturalists, but was now destined to become a flourishing town since the development of a harbour for freighters and super-tankers. It was also a place destined to cater for the beauty needs and moods of women.

By the time she had completed her business in

Richards Bay, a strong wind was blowing in clouds from the sea, which now had a more threatening look about it. Well, she thought, that was to be expected since, according to the news on the radio in her car, there was a cyclone off Madagascar and Natal could well have to face up to the whiplash. The cyclone was reported to be moving closer to the shores of Moçambique which, after all, was not so far off, as the crow flies. Still, it was unsettling, because if Ferdi did ring this evening while she was not at home, she would be terribly disappointed.

As Kristen drove on, kilometre after kilometre, even the black ribbon of road looked ominous and the weather continued to taunt her until the inevitable moment arrived when she was forced to think along the lines of stopping to buy food to take along to Holly's beach house at Surprise Bay. It had started to rain and there were increasing claps of thunder, followed by unnerving flashes of lightning. She pulled over to the side of the road, got out of her car and began running towards the small roadside supermarket and shopping complex which lay just off the National Road. She was relieved to recall that the dirt road which had led to Surprise Bay until only a short time ago was now a thing of the past—for it had just recently been tarred, after long months of confused bureaucratic wrangling.

She chose a small steak and then went to seek out anything which would serve to make a salad, and after putting these purchases into her car, she dashed back to a tiny gift shop where she had become known to the young woman who owned it.

'Hi, Kristen. More silk flowers?'

This had become quite a joke, and Kristen laughed.

'How did you guess? Julia, just give me that whole basket of flowers. I've no time to sort anything out.'

'Kristen, there are three dozen assorted silk flowers in there. Do you still want to take the basket?'

'Yes, I do. It doesn't matter.' Kristen was busy with her purse.

'The Lathbury beach house must look like a florist's shop,' Julia went on.

'It does,' Kristen answered, counting loose change to make up the amount of the flowers, 'but they look very attractive there. They look so realistic and always give the house a welcoming atmosphere. It's just my way of saying thank you for the use of the house. Holly—that is, Miss Lathbury—is very taken by them, even though she's an active Garden Club member. There's no flower garden at Salt Air, you see—only shrubs, lawns and trees.'

By the time she reached the beach house Kristen's whole body was tingling with nerves. She did not relish the idea of being alone in such a violent storm. Lightning forked across the sky, followed by crashing thunder which made her cringe.

The house appeared much larger than it was, being long and narrow. There were only two bedrooms, with adjoining bathrooms and, facing the sea, a long veranda ran the full length of the building. All the rooms could be opened to the sea-breezes by means of four huge sliding doors.

As she parked the Mazda in the carport, which was for guests, she hoped the car would not be blown away, because the wind was coming in from the sea in great savage gusts. The weather seemed to have gone completely mad, she thought, as she gathered some of her possessions together and then made a dash for it.

She would have to make two trips if she wanted to get everything into the house.

The bougainvillaea, which grew in profusion, was being blown to bits and on the veranda the potted plants which hung from the rafters were swinging about dangerously. After going to the car for the rest of her luggage she was panting for breath by the time she ran back up the steps to the veranda. Hugging the basket of assorted silk flowers, she began searching for the key, which was in her bag, and was cursing herself for not having done this while she was still in the car when the sliding doors to the living-room slid back and she looked up to see Nick Lathbury standing there. At the sight of him, she suddenly felt relieved and out of control, all at once. He was staggeringly handsome and for a moment his face registered shock. 'What the hell are you doing here? Never mind, come inside, before we get blown away.'

Kristen stood helplessly, for a moment, watching him as he picked up her bag, parcels and attaché case, and then, when they were inside and he had closed the doors, she demanded, 'What are *you* doing here?' With her beautiful golden-green eyes still on him, she shifted the position of the basket of multi-coloured flowers, but she still had to look over the top and the flowers almost framed her face.

'Personally, that's exactly what I'm thinking about you,' he said. 'What brings *you* here, for God's sake? Why do you have to turn up to complicate matters?'

'I didn't anticipate finding you here.' She went on staring at him in bewilderment.

'No?' He gave her a disbelieving look as he passed her on his way to the kitchen with the groceries she had brought along. She waited for him to come back and then watched him as he put his hands on his hips and went on looking at her.

'Obviously, I'll have to leave,' she said, blinking.

His dark-blue eyes went over her black linen suit and white flouncy blouse, before going to her overnight bag which was on the floor where he had dropped it.

'Obviously you came to stay, though. Right?' There was a hard edge to his voice.

'You don't understand,' she started to say, but he cut in quickly.

'Oh, cool it, Kristen! I think I understand very well. You've already been to work on my aunt and now you're about to get to work on me, is that it?'

She was devastated. 'I just don't understand this. Holly has given me permission to use this house in an emergency,' she told him, her voice beginning to rise. 'She had a key cut.'

Nick went on looking at her. 'And so this is an emergency?'

'Well, what the hell do you think?' Her eyes went to the glass doors and the wildness beyond.

'Something like the hole in the wall, in other words?'

'I don't know what you're talking about. What hole in the wall?' She could not see where this was leading.

'The emergency door in the corridor—what else? The door which is always left unlocked so that you have access to my aunt's home whenever you feel the inclination to insinuate yourself into her affections!'

'How dare you talk to me like this?' Her voice rose. 'What a disgusting thing to say!'

'Where have you come from—all dolled up like this?' His eyes went over her.

'I don't really have to explain anything to you—but as you've asked, I've come from Richards Bay. This is simply because I happen to be a representative for House of Marini and because my work revolves around the sales and promotion, not to mention the publicity, of an extensive range of beauty preparations. I'm not here by choice, Mr Lathbury.' Her voice was scathing. 'But let me go on, to put your incredible mind to rest. In my work, I often find myself compelled to put up at motels if, for some reason or another, I can't make the trip in one day. There's no mystery to my turning up here—and by the way, I didn't have to go to work on your aunt, she *insisted* that I have a key. She said to look on Salt Air as my own since it's nearly always unoccupied. She always lets me know when it's occupied. A little while ago, for example, some Garden Club ladies stayed here for four days.'

He laughed at that, but it was not a pleasant sound. 'That was very generous of her—but then Holly is more than generous, as you well know. And so here you are, like Kuan-Yin, bearing a basket-load of silk flowers to Salt Air? A wide assortment of every fascinating hue under the sun. There's even, I see, a flaunting cactus.'

With considerable heat she said, 'I haven't the slightest idea who Kuan-Yin happens—or happened— to be. Suppose you get to the point?'

'Kuan-Yin is a goddess of mercy,' he answered, while his dark blue eyes went over her.

'Why should *I* be compared to a goddess of mercy, after the wild reception I've just had?' Suddenly Kristen realised she was still holding the basket of flowers, and she bent down and put the basket on the carpet, next to one of the sofas.

'Work it out for yourself . . . apart from anything else, you'll help to break the boredom around here.' The remark, she knew, was a calculated insult, and a wave of troubled confusion washed over her.

'So you think I've come to flaunt myself before your eyes? It's frightening how coarse you can be! I resent that, and it's just not fair. Why are you keeping on at me like this?'

'Why, indeed?' There was contempt in his eyes. 'By the way,' he went on, 'I came here to get quietly drunk, so be prepared for that. I'm already on the way. There's food to eat and lots to drink, so make yourself at home. I find, after all, that I can easily adjust to having you here.'

'Well, you'd better re-adjust because I'm going,' she told him, and felt sheer despair at the thought of having to go back into the storm. 'Do you imagine that because I allowed you to kiss me the other night, it gives you the right to make disgusting remarks to me? Do you think this ring gives you the right to treat me like a common thief?' She slipped the ring of garnets and pearls from her finger and held it in the palm of her hand. 'I have no intention of staying in this house.' She slipped the ring back on her finger and turned away from him—then caught her breath when he took her by the shoulders.

'You'll stay here. It would be madness to leave now. What are you trying to prove? That, contrary to what it looks like, you're a very nice girl?' His blue eyes probed hers. 'Quite apart from anything, do you think I'm going to stand by and let you go out into that mess? Listen to the rain and the wind!'

Beyond the glass, the sky was a turbulent mass of black clouds, blowing in from the sea which, along with the beach and sand-dunes, was almost obliterated from view by driving rain. It was a wild and menacing picture, and she knew she would not get very far, once she left the house.

After giving her a long speculative look Nick said, 'Which bedroom would you like?' His voice was suggestive and he succeeded in insulting and humiliating her once again. She lifted her hands and shoved them through her hair.

'Am I going to live through this? I think I'm beginning to come apart at the seams! Right now, it's incredible to think you're Holly's nephew.'

'You might as well know,' he told her, 'I've had a row with Holly. It's left me feeling sick.'

Kristen watched him as he moved away from her and began to turn on the lamps. Immediately, the room with its golden-hued split-pole ceiling looked more inviting. The lamps highlighted the ceiling and the paintings which were mostly of flowers and hung to create an element of fresh homeliness. A tall antique cabinet, reaching almost to the ceiling, held books.

A flash of lightning seemed to explode right beside Kristen and she jumped, putting her fingers to her mouth, then remained standing transfixed while she watched Nick lift her cases and go in the direction of the bedrooms.

When he came back he said, in a friendlier voice, 'I've put your things in the one with the towering palm. Who the devil put that in there? Do you know?'

'No, I don't.' Her expression was accusing and miserable. 'Perhaps Holly had it brought here. As you know, the caretaker and his wife see to everything, including the plants.' As it happened, the caretaker was a relative of Micky Naidoo, Holly's driver. After a moment she asked, 'Why did you and Holly quarrel, Nick?'

'Give a little thought to it,' he answered, 'while you're here. You never know, it might just come to you.'

'Oh, so we're back on *that* again?' She expelled a long breath. 'Oh, Nick, I'm so sick of all this that I'm beginning to feel I'd like to throw this—this bloody ring in the sea!'

'You've caused a lot of trouble, Miss Ashton.' He shook his head and took a long breath. His voice was surprisingly gentle, but there was undisguised anger in his blue eyes.

'Apparently!'

'But some things remain the same,' he added.

'Such as?' Her golden-green eyes were accusing.

'Such as my still wanting to make love to you.'

She felt excited but, at the same time, dismayed. 'That's hardly likely to happen.'

Turning from her, he said, 'I wondered who was reponsible for all the flowers.'

To hide her confusion and the fact that she was close to tears she said, 'I hope they don't affront your big macho image?'

'Oh,' he shrugged, 'I can live with them. Anyway, you'd better get settled, because you're here to stay. You've no choice about it. This storm is going to have to blow itself out. When you've done that, we'll think about having something to eat.'

'I suppose there's nothing else I can do,' she answered. 'I brought a steak—not very big—and there are things for a salad.'

He laughed. 'I have enough food here to withstand a siege, and the bar is well stocked, I promise you.'

'I'm not interested in your bar,' she snapped. '*I'm* not here to get quietly drunk!'

'Well, that's fine with me, too.' Nick shrugged indifferently. 'I'll grill the steak if you make a salad. Since we're about to suffer this storm together, we might as well make the best of it.'

Growing more tense with each second, Kristen began to take off her black linen jacket which was damp and, looking at it, she saw it would need careful hanging. The white blouse, with its high neck and frilled jabot, was at once both demure and provocative, outlining her small breasts and drawing attention to her slim shoulders.

'I'll be back in a moment,' she said, and walked into the bedroom, where she changed into the black trousers which formed the third garment to the suit. These were the kind of clothes she bought. Slipping out of the white frilly blouse, she put on a skimpy black top with shoelace straps.

The storm seemed to be growing worse with each minute, and she was thankful that Nick was here, even though he had gone out of his way to insult and humiliate her and would probably go on doing so. She felt a spurt of sheer fury towards Holly for having gone out of her way to show Barbro up by holding her as a shining example. No wonder Nick was so mad!

Feeling self-conscious and miserable, she went through to the kitchen. Nick was already grilling the pieces of steak and each time he lifted one of them to turn it, there was a loud sizzle as it came down on the grill.

'I'll set the table first,' she said, and left the kitchen to go to the dining-room where she began to put place-mats on the knotty pine country-style table.

Here again, there were silk flowers put there by her on one of her stop-overs. She had arranged eight small white vases with silk mauve and white stocks which looked as beautiful as real flowers and looked stunning on the knotty pine dresser with blue and white porcelain on it. The knotty pine had the patina of a collector's piece.

Going back to the kitchen, she washed lettuce and tomatoes and while she was busy making the salad Nick said, 'I've brought an excellent vintage along— and by the way, I don't mean a vintage car.'

She thought it best to let that slide and replied, 'Well, you didn't expect to share it, so I'll put only one glass on the table.' Her voice was cool.

'You underestimate me,' he told her. 'Do you think I only brought one bottle along?'

She watched him moodily as he went to a cupboard and took out two green-stemmed crystal glasses. 'They're about a hundred years old,' he said. He seemed to exude vitality and sex appeal.

After everything had been prepared they went through to the dining-room. It was not quite dark and they could see the lashing curtains of rain and high waves, on the nearby shore and the spray which was being blown from the mountainous crests.

Silence hung between them and as Kristen went on eating she was aware that Nick often looked at her in this new hostile awareness. Lifting her eyes suddenly, she was immediately stunned at the threat in his. Raising the tall green-stemmed glass to his lips, he went on studying her over the rim while she tried to translate the look and what it stood for. She could not decide whether it was one of puzzlement or admiration.

Another bolt of lightning caused her to catch her breath. 'It feels as if the roof is coming off,' she shuddered. 'This is really hideous!'

Ignoring her comment, Nick observed, 'You must have seemed like a gift from heaven when you came into Holly's life.'

'You've said that before.' Her voice was hostile. 'Oh, Nick, don't try to heap guilt on me. I've done very little to warrant all this.'

'You reckon?' He looked at her with faint amusement.

'You know,' she looked up and their eyes met, 'I'd begun to psych myself into believing that you really meant it when you said you didn't care about the ring but you do, don't you? Along with the vintage car!'

'Don't remind me about the vintage car,' he growled. There was a glint of angry humour in his blue eyes.

After the meal he helped her to stack the dishes in the dishwasher, then he said, 'I feel like some Irish coffee.'

'I don't know how to make it,' she answered stiffly.

'I'm an expert. Go through and I'll bring you one presently.'

Although she was terrified of the storm, she left him and went through to the living-room. The curtains had not been drawn and she could see the rain pouring down relentlessly and washing in, drenching the long veranda, splashing over the rustic eating-out furniture. Baskets of ferns and other plants swung violently from the ceiling beams and she heard a crash as one fell at the far end. The whole scene was lit up, from time to time, by flashes of lightning, and she cringed as she went to draw the curtains.

She turned quickly as Nick came into the room with the Irish coffees and she felt apprehensive and unhappy as she saw him put the glasses down on the table between the two sofas. His thoughts were impossible to gauge from his expression.

'So,' he said, 'were it not for my aunt having asked you to move into the flat, I would never have met you.' She could detect the sarcasm in his words.

'I'd like you to know that I'm paying rent for the flat,' she retorted. 'Just in case your mind is festering in *that* direction. I'm paying quite a hefty rent, if it comes to that.'

His eyes met hers. 'But it's worth the high rent. Right?'

'Well, of course. I love the flat and I adore Holly.'

'I'm sure you do.'

'Is that what's bothering you?' she asked furiously.

'That—and a lot of other things.' He went on holding her gaze.

'To put your mind at rest,' she went on, 'I pay my rent regularly and the furniture is my own.'

'With a few exceptions, of course!' Nick lifted the Irish coffee glass to his mouth.

'Well . . . yes. I'm storing a few bits and pieces, of course.'

The angry mockery was there again. 'Storing them for whom, Kristen?'

Deciding, in her rage, to use the calm efficient tone she used in her cosmetic representative routine, she asked, 'Suppose you tell me what's on your mind? There *is* something on your mind, isn't there?'

'You know that,' he answered. 'The biggest thing on my mind right now is that I want to make love to you.' He put his glass down and then lowered himself to the sofa opposite her, while Kristen sat back amongst the cushions and stared at him in angry bewilderment.

'Really? And yet you went out of your way to brush me off, after succeeding in getting me to lose my head, after the Prentices' party.'

'Let's just say that where you're concerned I anticipated running into problems—and I did.' He gave her a level look.

'Oh, you did?' Her voice was sneering now. 'With Barbro, of course? You've also had a row with Barbro, right?'

He laughed lightly. 'Barbro is the least of my worries right now. Anyway, let's change the subject. So you like this house?' He glanced around the room.

'Yes.' Her voice was sulky. 'Actually, I've been here so often in the last three months, I'm beginning to feel I own it.'

'I'm sure,' he said. 'Tell me about your brother's wedding.'

'Are you really interested?' Kristen was beginning to lose patience. 'You said Holly had written to you about it and she also sent you a newspaper cutting. What else do you want to know? Or are you just trying to ruffle me?'

'I'm really interested,' he answered.

'Well,' she thought for a moment, 'the church was massed with flowers.' Her voice was sarcastic.

'From Holly's garden . . . go on . . .'

'Not *all* from Holly's garden, Nick! *Some*.' She was livid now. 'What is this—and who told you the flowers came from the garden?'

'If you must know . . . Barbro. She wrote to me about it.'

'Oh, I see.' She sat back fuming.

'Go on,' he said. 'We've got to talk about something.'

'Libby . . . the bride wore an exquisite gown and her veil seemed to float.' She felt a sudden need to scream.

'Was it new, or was it—something—borrowed?' he asked, casually enough.

'It was new, and her bouquet, *not* from Holly's garden, but from a well-known florist, was in shades of pink, blue and the most delicate bronze.' She took a furious little breath. '*But* . . . what you're really waiting to hear is that Micky Naidoo drove Libby to the flower-massed church and then on to the reception in Holly's veteran car—which, I've come to the conclusion, bothers you very, very much. Holly was terribly kind.'

'As I well know from personal experience, Holly can be very kind when you get to work on her,' answered Nick, and, listening to him, Kristen felt threatened because Nick Lathbury had, quite definitely, become an enemy.

'I didn't have to go to work on her—neither did Craig and Libby. You're deliberately misunderstanding me and—by the way, *I* didn't design that Christmas card. Just bear that in mind.'

'I'm aware of the Christmas card in question,' he replied shortly. 'I've heard about nothing else since I got back—along with a whole host of other things.'

'Have you quite finished interrogating me?' she asked angrily.

'I've barely started,' he answered easily. 'One small thing, Kristen, a veteran car is a car built prior to December the thirty-first, 1918. I believe cars built prior to December the thirty-first 1904, are regarded as true veterans and are eligible to take part in the world-famous Brighton Run. The others are known as Edwardian veterans, and cars built after that period, but before the end of 1930, are vintage, a term often confused with veteran. So what does that make Holly's car—certainly not veteran and, I should imagine, certainly not vintage—but then I might be wrong. My interest doesn't stretch that far, but I do happen to be attached to the old bus. Maybe, in a few moments, we'd better drink a toast to it. Such appreciation all round, Barbro included, should be rewarded.'

There was a hostile silence in the room while, outside, the storm raged on and on, tightening Kristen's nerves even more.

'Go and tell Barbro all this,' she said. 'She's the one who's trying to get her hands on Holly's car.'

'There's not much chance of that, is there? Not with *you* fawning over Holly.'

'Look,' she said angrily, 'I don't think I have to account—and go on accounting—to you for my relationship with Holly. Damn it, it's not something you have to develop a drinking problem over, surely? That's pretty pathetic, really!' Her voice was a little wild now.

'There's not a chance of my developing a drinking problem, Kristen.' His voice was very quiet and his blue eyes were hard and seemed to pierce right through her.

Watching him with baffled eyes, she felt at an utter loss to understand his chilling attitude towards her.

'I keep trying to understand you—but I give up. What is it with you, anyway? We didn't *scratch* the damn car.' She took a breath. 'And ... about Holly.

You just don't understand her—honestly . . .' Her voice trailed away.

'I understand her very well. After all, she brought me up. I regard her as my mother—but let me tell you one thing, my father's sister was not nicknamed prickly Holly for nothing.'

'I can't imagine she was called prickly Holly,' Kristen retorted sharply. 'Holly also happens to be an evergreen shrub with exquisite small white flowers. It also bears beautiful red berries. You really are the limit—and I don't want to hear another thing!' Nick's remark, however, had set her thinking, but she would never let him know this. Was this the real reason Miss Elizabeth Lathbury had been given the nickname, all those years ago? She had grown to learn that Holly had a sweet disposition when she got her way, which was often, when one came to think about it.

'You can't love your aunt very much,' she said angrily.

'I love her very much, as it happens. I also happen to worry about her, very much. You see, I've grown to learn that she can be very vulnerable, one way and another.' Suddenly he laughed lightly. 'I'm giving you a hard time, Kristen, aren't I?'

She watched him, with wide eyes, as he stood up and came over to where she was sitting. When he took her hand and pulled her up beside him, they were standing very close together, and Kristen was shocked and disgusted with herself to discover that his touch was like an electric shock. She felt overpowered by him, and when he put his arms about her and traced her spine with his fingers, she found herself holding her breath, her eyes clinging to his.

After a moment he said, very softly, 'You've been so

nice to my aunt, why not be nice to me? You never know, it might pay off.'

The rain was battering the sliding glass doors and windows in the house and the thunder and lightning had not ceased, and for a moment, she wondered if she had heard Nick correctly.

'What are you trying to say to me?' she asked, in a stifled voice.

'You intrigue me,' he told her, 'very much. I happen to want you—very much.'

For a moment she struggled against him, yet when he bent his head and touched his mouth to hers she found she wanted to respond to him . . . and that she was. Perhaps the storm had something to do with it, she found herself thinking. His arms tightened about her and it was like putting a flame to a fuse, and her arms went up to his shoulders.

'My aunt was a push-over,' he whispered, 'and I guess that goes for me too.'

He slid his hands down the length of her back and they came to rest on her small buttocks. He crushed her body against his own, moving against her, and a weakness seemed to invade her, but it was a weakness that did not prevent her from clinging to him.

Outside the beach house, the wind was at its peak and there was the sound of crashing, as another potted fern was wrenched from its position on one of the veranda roof beams and hurled to the floor. Nick swore under his breath but went on kissing her.

'Perhaps we should explore this,' he said softly, 'some place else . . . What do you say?'

Before she quite knew what was happening he had picked her up, and there was a sense of unreality about the whole situation, she thought, as she tried to handle it without looking like a heroine of the silent silver screen.

With a sickening shock she realised that Nick was carrying her in the direction of the bedroom with the potted palm, and then, as he lowered her to the bed and cupped her face in both hands, their lips were meeting and she moved closer against him.

After a moment he drew back from her. 'What are you saying?'

Although she had not spoken she came to her senses immediately. 'I think you know what I'm saying, Nick. I'm saying *no*!'

When she tried to get up, however, he pushed her back against the pillows. His thighs were against her own, and although she felt desire flooding her, she said softly, 'Damn you! You don't seriously believe I'll go to bed with you?' She gave a choked sob as he ignored her and his fingers stroked her ears, thrilling nerves she hadn't expected to find there. Beneath his chest, her nipples were taut and a sure betrayal of her response to him. Her hands went to the back of his neck and travelled up to his dark hair. Wanting him so desperately, at this moment, was far more violent, far more terrifying, than the storm that raged outside.

Nick tried to make the kiss more intimate, but she shook her head from side to side. 'No.' She spoke from behind clenched teeth.

'Why not?' His voice was urgent.

'Because I don't want you to. This is crazy!'

'I don't think so. You protest because you think it's expected of you to protest. It's a behaviour pattern . . . forget it, Kristen.'

When she could free her lips to answer him she said,

'And you can forget about the psycho-analysis, Nick. I have no intention of letting this happen.'

'I've come under your spell,' he told her. 'I can't say I blame Holly . . . she was a sitting duck, and so am I.'

'You're making that up, aren't you, just to . . . well . . . just to get me into bed with you! Don't make me mad, Nick. Believe it or not, I haven't spent a night with Ferdi.'

'Don't talk to me about that character in Gstaad,' he answered, nuzzling his lips against her neck. 'I'm not interested.'

'In any case,' she moved her head, 'I've never permitted myself to indulge in dangerous—what I'm trying to say is that I've never *wanted* to get involved—this way . . .'

As he stroked her hair back from her forehead he drew back and his blue eyes watched the movements of his own hands, then, after a long silence, he said, 'You're beautiful. I want you so much—you know that. Do you want me to go on?'

Kristen was beginning to sense her vulnerability and, at the same time, she realised that her answer could be a landmine. She said honestly, 'Yes—and no. I've told you about the no part—but I guess you're more than aware of the yes part.'

'More yes than no?' The words were very soft.

'Yes.' Her golden-green eyes searching his anxiously. 'Yes, if you must know, but I'm not willing to take the chance.'

Nick began to caress her arm, then he picked up her hand and kissed her palm, stroking the centre of it with his tongue and sending shock-waves through all the secret places of her body. He transferred his lips to her ears and kissed them and she knew he was tantalising her.

'Nice little perfumed ears,' he whispered, and when she closed her eyes he kissed her eyelids and then moved on to her mouth. She opened her eyes and looked at him; his eyes were questioning. I'm floundering, she thought, but she was determined not to show it. What are you trying to do to yourself . . .

'Put your arms round me, Kristen.' It was a command.

Vaguely, she was aware of the roar of the surf and the wind as it shook the house to the very foundations. As her arms went round Nick she was aghast at her lack of control, and in an attempt to overcome her emotions she dropped her arms to her sides, and as she did so, her engagement ring caught in the woven bedcover. When she tried to free it this only exacerbated the matter.

Nick tried to pull her closer to him and in a wave of humiliation, she murmured, 'Something's caught.'

When he ignored her she said, 'I can't move. Something is caught.'

He made no attempt to release her and went on kissing her breasts through the material of her black top, and though she could feel his moist breath around her nipples she knew he was beginning to get angry.

'Nick, damn you! My ring! The setting is caught in the material.' As she spoke the words she felt the chill of despair.

His anger beginning to spiral, he snapped, 'Well, take the bloody thing off, then.' He tried to do this himself by reaching to where her hand was. Suddenly the ring came off her fingers, but it had remained caught in the woven material. Immediately she covered her face with her hands and was aware of Nick moving away from her, before he rolled off the bed.

After a moment she heard him say, 'Finding you desirable, my beautiful con-woman, poses a mass of problems . . .'

She sat up immediately. 'What kind of remark is that?' she demanded. 'A con is a swindler! Damn you! How dare you?' She lifted a pillow and hurled it across the room but he had already gone.

CHAPTER FOUR

IT poured all night and water poured from roof gutterings which could not cope with the deluge. There was little relief from the howling of the wind, and this, along with the water noises and the roar of the surf, made sleep for Kristen impossible.

During the seemingly endless hours, she tossed and turned. When she wasn't concentrating on the violence of the storm, she was thinking about Ferdi, Nick Lathbury, Holly . . . and a woman named Barbro who, believing Nick had not got back for Christmas, had cleared off somewhere—to get even, no doubt.

Wearing the same black slacks and shoulder-strapped top she had worn the night before, Kristen was up and about before Nick, with the intention of leaving Salt Air as soon as possible.

She had made coffee and was sipping some in the kitchen when Nick arrived on the scene, and looking at him, she realised that while she had believed he was still in bed he had, in fact, been out in the rain.

Shrugging out of his raincoat, he said, 'I trust you managed to sleep through that racket last night?' There was a flint-like hardness about him and as she lifted the coffee-mug to her lips her hand shook.

'I did *not* sleep well, as it happens—but *you* saw to that, didn't you? How dare you call me a con-woman? You called me a flaunting cactus. That was bad enough!'

Nick held her look for a moment, then turned away.

'Kristen,' he said, 'I've been up to the small bridge. I expected to find it washed away, actually, but it's still standing, although it's partly submerged. Partly . . .' he turned again to look at her, 'but dangerously so.'

'Will I be able to drive across it?' she asked. 'I want to leave here as soon as possible. I've had enough.'

His dark blue eyes were impenetrable and moody as they rested on her face. 'You're not going to be able to leave, so resign yourself to that. The water level will have to go down, and that will only happen some time after the rain has stopped.'

'What are we going to do?' she asked, as she lowered the mug to the saucer. 'This poses more problems.'

'Don't include me in this.' He spoke with callous indifference. 'Since *I* don't intend leaving here it makes absolutely no difference.'

Kristen watched him with angry eyes as he began pouring himself a mug of coffee. Looking up, suddenly, and catching her unawares he said, 'So, what are you scheming *now*?'

'If you must know, I've just been trying to work out how I can kill myself.' Her voice barely contained her frustrated anger. 'I'm furious with you! Not only have you said some outrageous things about me, you've also said some nasty things about Holly which I resent very much!'

She followed him with her eyes as he walked over to her. 'I don't blame you for coming to Holly's defence.' His blue eyes had lost none of their chill. 'She thinks the world of you, after all. You've made a friend for life, believe me.'

Listening to him with mounting fury, she retorted,

'For that matter, Nick, she thinks the world of you too.'

He shrugged his shoulders which, even though he had been wearing a raincoat, were damp. 'Well, I guess that's simple enough to explain. I *am* her world, after all—or rather, I've always believed myself to be. There are just the two of us. I lost my parents in a senseless accident and I lived in that house with Holly, on and off, taking into account my school and Varsity days. She brought me up. I'm like the son she never had and she's like a mother to me. Make no mistake, I love her very much.'

Because she was hurt and angry Kristen said childishly, 'You're not the only one who's lost parents in a senseless accident.' She glanced down at the ring of garnets and pearls, and the ring appeared to be blurred and double on her finger.

'I didn't say I was, Kristen!' he exploded. 'Don't get sidetracked!'

'When I get back to the flat,' she told him, 'I intend explaining to Holly that I can't keep this ring. It really bugs you, doesn't it? That and the fact that Craig had use of the vintage car on his wedding day—not to mention that I'm staying in the Lathbury mansion.'

'I've already told you—I'm not interested in the ring, Kristen. Keep it. Right now, the ring is the very last thing on my mind.'

'Well, what is on your mind?' Her expression was sullen and hostile. 'If it's not the ring or the car—what is it?'

'Forget it,' he snapped.

'No! I want to know!'

Nick took a breath and expelled it. 'Okay.' He spread his hands. 'You. You. You! All round . . . from every angle. One way and another you're the focal point of my mind. I feel as if I've been shot between my eyes. When I was in England and Holly wrote telling me about you and sent me the newspaper cuttings of your brother's wedding. I wondered what you'd be like, it didn't take me long to find out that you're a very beautiful and desirable con-woman. Do you imagine the violent elements of the cyclone are on my mind?'

'If you call me a con-woman once more, I'll throw something at you! The trouble with you is that you're as mad as a snake that Holly doesn't like Barbro, which, incidentally, has nothing to do with me ... and, talking about being beautiful and desirable, I guess you would have found any woman desirable in these circumstances. Perhaps you've been making passes at me because your precious Barbro couldn't wait long enough to see whether you managed to hop on a plane at the last minute?'

'Let's face it—you seemed to be enjoying yourself,' he said coldly.

'I was an idiot, and you ... well, you were on an ego trip. You're so sure of yourself, aren't you? You think you have everything going for you to make it with me. Well, you have less power, Nick Lathbury, than you damn well imagine!' After a moment Kristen added despairingly, 'Put it all down to this wretched cyclone.'

'Put it down to something else.' His voice was hard. 'Forget about the so-called ego trip and put it down to what it really is—pure physical attraction. Indeed, to go one step more—*mutual* physical attraction.'

Their eyes met and she shook her head. 'Physical attraction isn't something I want to enjoy at random, and certainly not with you!'

'No?' He laughed softly. 'Kristen, my sixth sense told me I'd find you to be a disruptive force, but I hadn't counted on just how much.' He put his coffee mug down on the counter and came over to her, and then, before she could stop him, he put his arms about her and began stroking the back of her neck with his fingers, while his eyes held hers. His hands went to her hair and he drew his fingers through it before they continued down the nape of her neck, thrilling the nerves there.

'I'm a disruptive force because, unfortunately, Holly has gone out of her way to show you that she likes me, whereas there's this antagonism towards Barbro,' she answered.

'Let's not drag Barbro into this again,' he told her shortly. 'After all, you're the one who's turning the world upside down right now.' His arms tightened and he drew her closer, but she pushed him away.

'I want to leave here in about ten minutes' time,' she snapped, 'just as soon as I get my things together, in other words.'

'So you're determined to risk the elements?' queried Nick.

'Yes, I am—and nothing's going to stop me. I'll manage somehow—even if I have to swim!'

'So you're leaving me here with the silk flowers?' His voice contained mockery. 'I'll have to take one to bed with me tonight.'

'Well, do that. *I* don't have *that* problem.' Her remark was pointed. 'In other words, I don't feel the need to take someone to bed with me.'

Suddenly he was angry again. 'Kristen, there's no way you can leave here. The water is above the bridge now, and that's the truth, whether you believe it, or not.'

Kristen shook her hair back from her cheeks. 'I don't care. I'm going to try.'

'I have no intention of allowing you to try.' His blue eyes were blazing now.

'How am I to know you're not stringing me along?' she asked.

'I'll drive you there,' he told her. 'That way, you can see for yourself. Get your raincoat.'

A few moments later they went out to a world of swirling rain, and when she got into Nick's dark green Jaguar she felt she had entered a protected world of soft, honey-hued leather.

They did not talk as they drove through the rain in the direction of the bridge. Nick drove to a spot where they could look down on what was visible of the bridge, which amounted to the top railing. Rain drummed on the roof of the car and distorted everything in view.

Turning to look at her, he asked, 'Are you satisfied?'

'Yes,' she replied quickly. 'I have no option.'

'Okay. Let's make the best of a bad job. We'll go back to Salt Air, silk flowers and champagne. In fact, we'll have a champagne breakfast.' There was a hint of a smile on his face, and she turned away and bit her lip.

'What will we be celebrating?' she asked, after a moment, her voice heavy with sarcasm.

'The beginning of our affair.' Nick glanced at her, then started the car and turned it and headed back in the direction of the beach house.

'Put it on record, there will be no affair,' Kristen retorted. 'And another thing—you go on and on about those silk flowers. Holly likes them, and that's the main thing. I put them there for Holly—and her friends—when they visit the house. Besides, they're not cheap, trashy things. They're exquisite—made in the Orient.'

'I didn't say I didn't like them, did I? I'm not complaining. In fact, they had me deceived when I arrived. After all, I hadn't seen them before. I thought they were real flowers.'

'As for that silly remark about starting an affair,' Kristen went on, 'so far as I'm concerned that's about a million-to-one against chance.'

'You reckon?' He laughed lightly. 'We'll see. Anyway, we'll work on it. I was thinking it might just solve a lot of things.'

'And, on the other hand, it may not.' She turned away and gazed out of the window, then shivered.

Directly they entered the house, she said stiffly, 'I noticed there are ingredients for making pancakes and I see there's bacon. I'll do pancakes and we'll have them with grilled bacon. By cooking for you I'll be working my way, as I have no food left. Okay?'

'Fine.' Nick shrugged off his raincoat and left her, and by the time he came into the kitchen again she was looking out the ingredients.

While she was busy mixing the pancake batter he said, 'I've been thinking. It would be to my advantage if this little episode ended with the triumphant strains of the *Lohengrin* Wedding March.'

'Really?' She felt absurdly excited by his remark, but vaguely, at the back of her mind, she realised he was only getting at her.

'I can picture your glorious face covered by exquisite drifts of Brussels lace. I believe Holly has a veil tucked away somewhere which probably belonged to my grandmother. Holly likes to keep things for ever, as you've probably noticed. I remember her showing Barbro the veil—before all the ill-feeling—and explaining that it was rich with seed pearls. Think of the coloured picture on the front page of the paper and the article to go with it . . . the bride and groom ran, laughing, through a shower of confetti towards Miss Elizabeth—better known as Holly—Lathbury's 1938 Morris Eight.'

'Oh, so we're back on the subject of Miss Elizabeth Lathbury's 1938 Morris Eight, are we?' Kristen's voice was scathing. Ignore him, she said to herself. After all, you can choose to be hurt, offended, hostile or humiliated, which is just what he wants, actually. So, give him a shot in the eye and keep your cool.

She looked out of the window at the rain and remained calm. 'Although this is a beach house,' she said, 'it's far from exciting on a day like this—especially when one happens to be with the wrong person, don't you think?'

Nick gave her a mocking glance. 'I don't know about that. You must admit we've got a lot going for us—champagne, flowers, food—and an inner struggle going on in you which could get out of hand.'

'Well, those things won't clothe me,' she retorted. 'I have no clothes here, dammit.'

He was grilling bacon and looked up. 'I should say you brought more than enough.' She felt the sarcasm and gave him an angry look.

'I think I explained that I always carry a few things. In my job I have to. I never know when I'm going to have to spend a night away from home.' She took a ruffled little breath. 'Order in my life is essential and that goes for my—my sex life too. Just bear that in mind.'

'Well, we'll change that,' he answered. 'Actually, although I've found you to be more than just a little responsive, it didn't take me long to discover that you've had little experience in the art of lovemaking. Now's your chance to learn.'

'I wasn't aware that I was seeking a teacher. Tell me, Nick you forgotten that you have a fiancé?' Her voice was scathing.

'When a man's fiancée happens to be a cheat there's no need to dwell on the fact.' He shrugged and then lifted his lashes to look at her again. 'Is there? We both happen to be in the same position, don't we?'

'I don't think so. Ferdi isn't a cheat.' Kristen began to beat the pancake mixture. 'There's no need to try and ruffle me just because you're annoyed about Barbro—because you are, aren't you?'

'What would you like to hear me say? That I feel screwed out of shape because of Barbro? Anyway, I'm not interested in a stroll down Memory Lane. I'm quite happy to be stranded here with a very desirable girl who has a skin like a golden apricot. That alone makes up for the lack of the honey-warmth of the sun.'

She began to make the pancakes, and when she had finished she popped them into the warming oven, leaving Nick to carry the breakfast things through to the living-room. Regardless of what she had said about the house being far from exciting on a day like this, the room was delightful with its long off-white canvas sofas and piled cushions in shades of emerald-green, crimson, coral and honey-gold. Even in dull weather the golden-split-pole ceiling seemed to glow and the modern paintings of flowers seem to swirl colour. The carpet was Persian, which always surprised her since the house was unoccupied most of the time.

On her way back to the kitchen she nearly bumped into Nick as he came through carrying a bottle of champagne which he carried loosely, almost carelessly, by the neck. As their eyes met she found herself wondering what the night would bring—and what it would be like having Nick make love to her, if she permitted him to.

Throughout breakfast he kept refilling her glass, and the champagne made her expansive.

'Do you know something?' she said. 'I suddenly find I'm in a very charitable mood. In other words, Nicholas, I've decided to make the best of a bad job and enjoy your company.' She laughed lightly and held out her glass when he reached for it, waiting until he had refilled it and then his own. 'I mean,' she lifted her shoulders, 'I agree with you. What's the point of being miserable when we can be happy? Cyclones can go on for days, can't they?'

'They run their course,' he answered.

'Exactly!' She settled back in the cushions and looked at him.

'So you've decided to be charitable?'

'Yes.'

'Does this mean I can expect the inevitable?' He surveyed her with an unfathomable expression.

'That doesn't deserve an answer,' she retorted.

After a moment he said, 'Talking about being charitable, up until a short time ago I'd always believed that charity begins at home.'

'Oh?' Kristen shrugged carelessly. 'I guess it doesn't really matter, just so long as it begins.' She laughed nonsensically.

He was wearing a dark blue shirt and white pants now, and these clothes emphasised and dramatised his good looks. He lolled back on one of the sofas, one arm flung carelessly along the back, and as Kristen gazed at him one word came to her mind—glamour. It was a word which did not only apply to women, she thought. Although he appeared relaxed, his body had lost none of the charismatic energy that had been one of the first things she had noticed about him.

Flustered all of a sudden, she turned away and gazed through the glass doors at the heaving sea and crashing, white-spumed surf, and shivered. Drinking champagne at this time of the day had made her more than just a little giddy. Well, in any case, it was more champagne than she had ever consumed at one time in her life.

To hide her confusion she got up and went to stand at the glass doors. The clouds continued to roll in from the sea, almost obscuring both it and the beach, but she could make out a lone seagull which was almost being blown along the sand. Without turning, she said, 'There's a seagull and the wind is so strong that the poor thing can't even get airborne, Nick. What will happen to it?'

'It will get by,' he told her. 'By the way, the fact that it can't fly is a warning if you happen to own a light plane. It means—don't try to take it up.'

'Well,' she swung round, 'I don't own a light plane. You're an unfeeling devil. How can you make light of that poor gull's predicament?'

'I'm not unfeeling.' He was angry now. 'What do you expect me to do, Kristen? By the time I struggled down to the beach it would have made its own plan. How else do you think they survive? What's the matter with you?'

She said nothing, but glanced down at Ferdi's ring

while she tried to understand her feelings about Nick. After a moment of brooding silence, she transferred her gaze to Holly's gift of garnets and pearls which, even in the grey light, seemed to glow with a hidden fire and, without realising she was doing so, she took a long, shuddering breath.

'Nick,' she said, without turning, 'this ring—from Holly—it was gift-wrapped when she gave it to me and I automatically thought it had come from that little antique shop—the one owned by her friend . . .' She broke off and turned to look at him.

His response was curt. 'Forget about the damn ring! I'm sick of hearing about it.'

Tension was building up again, so she began to clear away the blue and white plates and took them through to the kitchen where she began to stack them into the dishwasher.

'By the way,' said Nick behind her as he came into the kitchen, 'I listened to the news on my car radio, earlier on.'

'You didn't tell me.' Her voice was accusing. 'What was the news about the cyclone? I've been longing to know, and there's just a tape-deck in this house.'

'Well, I'm telling you now,' he snapped. 'It seems the rain has caused considerable damage, with rivers swollen and bridges washed away or under water. All this havoc is being created by the cyclone, which just happens to be pretty close to our own shores. Telephone lines are down, and it's remarkable that Surprise Bay still has power, actually. I just want you to get the picture.'

The picture, she thought, was that she was trapped here with him and with hardly any clothes, but, what was more important, she could well end up doing something painfully stupid, like going to bed with him, if he tried to make love to her again.

With nothing to do they went back to the living-room and after a few moments of stiff silence, Nick said, 'So you don't think Ferdi is cheating on you in Gstaad?'

'No, I don't.' She had been quick to notice that Nick's remark had contained cynical amusement.

'And you love him very much?' It was there again.

'Yes, I do. Not that it has anything to do with you.'

'How much?' He went on looking at her.

She shrugged. 'Very much.'

'Very much, huh? How can you be so madly in love with him and yet get sexually excited over me? It makes me feel you're not only a very clever, scheming girl but a wanton one as well.'

'I might ask you the same question,' she retorted. 'How can you be so madly in love with Barbro and yet get sexually excited over *me*?' Her golden-green eyes reflected his insult.

'It's a mixture of many things,' he answered lightly.

'You've got a nerve!' she exclaimed. 'I'm certainly not wanton. If I've appeared wanton it was for the simple reason that I felt strung up the moment I realised we were cut off here. I'm still strung up, as it happens.'

'Ah, so there's still hope?' He laughed softly.

'There is no hope, Nick. I've got myself very much under control.'

'You only think you have.' She saw his lazy eyes go to her long, trousered legs. 'Anything can happen—and you know it.'

'I'm not listening to this,' she said crossly. 'I have some work to do. My advice to you, Nick, is to leave me alone.'

After she had gone he began to play cassette music and, trying to gauge his mood, Kristen found herself concentrating on it. Because the light was so grey she had turned on the bedside lamps which stood on small chests on either side of the bed and the room was cast in a warm glow which was reflected in the honey tones of the split-pole ceiling.

She did not notice how long the music had stopped, for she had grown enthusiastic about making entries in a ledger from her attaché case. When she did become aware of the silence, she went through to the living-room and her eyes went immediately to the note Nick had left on the coffee table. 'I've gone out. Be back soon,' he had written on the back of a large envelope which was propped up against a small basket of silk flowers.

Her immediate reaction was one of resentment that he had gone out and left her behind to worry about him. No doubt, she found herself thinking, he had driven to the bridge again to see whether the water level had gone down.

Feeling unbearably depressed, Kristen decided to have a bath, then she slipped into the soft crimson caftan which always seemed to end up in her overnight case. Let Nick think what he liked, she thought, as she washed her underwear and hung it in the adjoining bathroom which served her room.

Kristen tidied her attaché case, which was so well organised that it didn't really need tidying. Everything she always needed was at her fingertips—credit card, chequebook, sunglasses and notebooks. By the time lunch time arrived and there was still no sign of Nick she began to fidget and worry and, to pass another hour, she made herself a cup of coffee and took it back to the living-room, trailing the soft crimson caftan as she walked in her flat gold slippers. Slipping them off, she lifted her legs to the sofa. Moodily she stared at the slanting rain, and as she listened to the wind, her worry and her resentment grew.

There were a number of novels in the glass-fronted bookcase and, choosing one, she tried to read, but found she could not concentrate. It was a very masculine novel and the characters revolved around heads of state, bankers and—unlikely to her way of thinking—the women behind the seats of power. After a while, she got up and picked out a cassette and the music helped to drown out the rain, wind and ocean noises, but she realised she had done the wrong thing in choosing classical music which, although absolutely beautiful, was hauntingly sad and influenced her mood.

It was almost dark when Nick got back, and one look at him told her that he was in a bad mood. After he had been to change out of very wet clothes he came back wearing his white pants and a black cashmere sweater with long sleeves.

For a while there was silence and she made a big show of reading, but when the silence became too much for her she said, 'Well, if it isn't himself! Did you see the bridge? What glad tidings do you have?'

She stiffened when she saw his eyes going over her crimson caftan and the gold slippers which she had dropped on to the Persian carpet.

'What does it matter?' He held her gaze.

'It matters a lot. I want to get away from here.'

'The water level is up,' he told her. 'The road into Surprise Bay is passable, though—the road leading in from Richards Bay end, that is. I was told that the only way out here is by going back about twelve kilometers and then linking up to the National Highway. In other words, when you decide to leave, that will be your route.'

'Really?' Her voice rose. 'When I *decide* to leave, you say? I've never been here of my own choice and you know it. What a pity you didn't come back with this piece of news earlier on. In that case I might have *decided* to leave then. If I leave now, what time do you think I'm going to get back to Durban tonight? That is, supposing I *make* Durban? How callous can you be? Anyway, I'll leave . . . if that's what you want.'

'Damn it, Kristen, I didn't come back because I was helping to rescue some people who'd been washed over a drift in their car. They were actually trapped in the car.' Nick pushed his fingers through his dark hair. 'I wasn't suggesting you go *now*, and you know it. I was merely passing on information about the condition of the roads.'

Kristen slipped her legs over the edge of the sofa and stood up, then bent down to pick up her gold slippers. 'I'm leaving,' she said.

'You are not, you know!' His voice was low and furious. The tension between them was thick. 'It's nearly dark, you little fool! In fact, visibility has been practically nil all day—or hadn't you noticed, sitting here all dolled up?' His eyes raked over her.

'Sitting here, in virtually the only change of clothing I have, Nicholas Lathbury, I *had* noticed, believe it or not, but I'm still determined to leave.'

'Like hell you are!' He came over to where she was standing and she saw the anger in his eyes.

'You left me sitting here worrying about you,' she snapped. 'Worrying how to find out where you'd gone and whether anything had happened to you. This is the whiplash of a cyclone, damn you, Nick, not just some three-day summer downpour. You could have been washed away and drowned, for all I knew.'

'Washed away and drowned! Well, that's beautiful, isn't it? That's really touching. Maybe it would have solved a whole lot of things if I had.'

'Oh, Nick, that really deserves a slap right across that sarcastic face of yours!' She turned her back on him, then swung round again. 'I mean . . .' she lifted her shoulders and her voice rose, 'why the hell should I want you to drown?'

He laughed outright in the way that never failed to anger her. 'You tell me, Kristen.'

Pushing past him, she went to the sliding glass doors where she stood looking at the dismal grey, swirling rain. She could hear the rain washing in, flooding the veranda, and then, lifting her arms, she said, 'This whole thing is so bizarre, it's unbelievable.' She turned to look at him. 'Being stranded here with you is not my idea of heaven, believe me. It was the very last thing I would have chosen for myself.'

'What *is* bizarre, Kristen, is that you created instant desire the moment I saw you when you arrived here. You'll never know how tantalisingly beautiful you looked, peering at me over your basket of silk flowers.'

'Flaunting cactus to match.' Her voice was scathing, but she felt something like panic because she realised she was in love with him. 'Oh well, that's your problem, not mine.'

'Look, let's stop this,' said Nick. 'Parts of the village are without electricity, so I suggest we make ourselves something to eat, while there's still the power to do it.'

'I don't intend eating,' she told him.

'Why not?'

'Just in case you've forgotten, the food I brought here happens to be finished, and I don't intend eating off you again, that's why.'

'If that's the way you feel then sit and watch me eat,' he told her, then he gripped her shoulders. 'Don't be so bloody childish, Kristen. What kind of remark is that?'

'Don't touch me!' she rasped. 'Take your hands off me!'

His blue eyes moved over her entire body and then focused on her eyes and mouth. 'You look very dramatic, very chic and very, very sexy. Where did *this* come from?' He lifted a fold of the crimson material.

'A travelling salesman gave it to me. I spent the entire day entertaining and being nice to him. Where the hell do you think it came from? Shut up! You make me so furious—I'm sick!'

Nick laughed softly. 'Oh, I'm not complaining, believe me, but you'd better be careful. Fury is a very debilitating emotion. To get back to food, though . . . I can offer you sausages, eggs and frozen oven-bake chips. You can toss a salad. I'll bet you've had nothing all day, right?'

Suddenly she was starving. 'What difference does it make?'

'It makes a big difference. I don't feel like eating alone. Now come on, snap out of it.' Kristen caught her breath when he swept her up and carried her in the direction of the kitchen. He stopped to kiss her on the mouth and she felt a surge of excitement.

When he put her down she said, 'My slippers—I dropped them—I must go and get them.'

By the time she returned to the kitchen Nick was already involved in grilling sausages. They worked together, and some time later, except for the eggs, everything was slipped into the warming oven and the salad into the refrigerator. Nick poured drinks, which they took through to the living-room, then Kristen watched him as he chose a cassette and tensed as the music began.

'Sit,' he said, turning. 'Relax. Let tomorrow take care of itself.'

She sat down and looked up at him from a huddle of jewel-coloured cushions, then she took the glass he was passing to her. Looking at his hands, she felt a surge of pure erotic sensation surging through her.

He had chosen a modern jazz cassette, and she was sensitive to the lingering notes of the piano and the whisper of brushes on drums.

A short while later her moody eyes followed him as he went back to the kitchen to pour more drinks, then she sat listening to the rain and the wind and tried to look casual when he came back.

'When do you plan to marry?' he asked, his gaze going to her engagement ring.

There was a small silence, then she said, 'Oh, soon. Soon . . . I'm not sure.' In the darkest corridors of her mind, though, she had a strong conviction that it would be never. Her feelings for Ferdi had shifted. She found herself wondering about the friends he had made in Gstaad—or was it *friend*?

'I don't want to discuss Ferdi right now,' she said, after a moment. 'I'm fed up with him, to be quite honest.'

'You're fed up and don't trust him. Right?'

Giving him an angry look, she snapped, 'Who says I

don't trust him? I trust him very much, as a matter of fact. It's just that I feel he *could* have got back for Christmas if he'd really tried.'

'After all . . . *I* got back.' Nick gave her a mocking glance. 'So you really trust him?'

'Yes. I said yes, didn't I?'

'And yet, the night I phoned from the airport, you seemed to be in the throes of an anxiety attack. I sensed it immediately, in fact.' He went on scrutinising her.

'Oh, that's nonsense,' she replied. 'If it sounded that way it was because I thought he was phoning from Gstaad and the call must be costing him a fortune. I wanted to get to the point quickly, and that was that I thought . . .' Her voice trailed away, then she went on, 'Look, I don't have to explain about Ferdi. What's more, I don't want to argue with you.' She gave him a level look. 'Does Holly know that—you know—that Barbro—about her, I mean . . .?'

'Holly has always considered Barbro to be a cheat, among other things.'

'But does she know you've—er—split up with Barbro?' She was feeling her way with him.

'Who says I've split up with her? She isn't even back yet.'

'Are you going to?' She gazed at him innocently.

'It depends.' He laughed softly. 'Why do you ask? Are stray thoughts beginning to trouble you?'

'Stray thoughts about—what?'

'About us. Be warned, Kristen, I usually get what I want.'

The lights flickered and she said, 'We still have the eggs to fry.' She put her glass down and stood up. 'I'll go and do them.'

They ate in the dining-room which, as always, looked welcoming with its knotty pine furniture and blue and white dishes and the plates on the wall. Conversation between them seemed to have dried up and there was an uneasy silence that seemed louder than the roar of the surf and the buffeting wind that shook the house. Kristen's mind was a blank and she tried to think of something to say.

'I wonder what kind of plates they are—on the wall, I mean,' she said, at last.

'Spode,' he answered.

'How do you know?' she asked.

'Why shouldn't I?' He went on looking at her, then he said, 'You'd better get used to the fact that I'm going to ask you to marry me. It will solve a lot of problems.'

Shaken, Kristen said as casually as she could, 'Why do you change the subject—and why don't you ask me now, so that I can say no and get it over with?'

'I'm keeping it for the right moment.' His blue eyes were mocking, but there was a hard look about his mouth.

'I didn't know you'd fallen in love with me,' she said, in what she hoped was a flippant tone. Her eyes locked with his. She felt distrust and disappointment and yet, at the same time, she felt a strange sense of excitement.

'Marriage doesn't always depend on being in love,' answered Nick, just as flippantly. 'What's more important is that we have an appreciation of the same things.'

'What, for instance?' Her experience cooled.

'Work it out. In any case, we both enjoy antiques,

we appreciate good paintings by good artists, we share an interest in good old-fashioned architecture.'

'I know nothing about architecture—old-fashioned or otherwise. You appear to be mixing me up with Barbro.'

Ignoring her remark, he went on, 'We both have an interest in vintage cars.'

'Again you're mixing me up with Barbro.' Kristen was working on overcoming her anger, but it was an effort. 'I can go on having an appreciation of all the things you've mentioned without entering into a farce of a marriage with you.'

'I have an idea that we'd excel at making love, once I'd taught you a few things, of course. If you're honest, you'll admit that this is what you had in mind right from the beginning.'

'I'd be a liar if I said I hadn't thought about how it would be to make love, but I don't intend—ever—to let that happen, so your snide remarks about marriage, Nick Lathbury, wash right over me.' Their eyes met over the flame of the candle which she had lit and placed in the centre of the table.

'Think about it,' he said.

'I have, and I think you've got a nerve, trying to get me into bed with you that way!'

Later, they went through to the living-room and Nick put on more music, but he seemed to be indifferent to it, while Kristen sat giving him resentful glances when she thought he wasn't looking.

When the big tree outside crashed down, fear spurred her reflexes and she almost shot from the sofa to where Nick was sprawled on the other sofa opposite.

Going down on her knees beside him, she said,

shakily, 'What's going on? This storm is too awful—will it never end?' Then she watched, with a kind of electric shiver of anticipation, as he leaned over and reached for her.

'It sounds like the old syringa tree,' he said. 'It's missed the overhead wires, thank God. What did you think it was?' He lifted a strand of her hair.

'I thought it might be the beginning of a tidal wave,' she said, beginning to feel the upheaval of her own private tidal wave as his arms closed about her, lifting her up.

With an easy movement Nick drew her up until they were lying side by side on the sofa, and with a fatalistic acceptance of what was in store for her, she made no resistance. She felt his body turn towards her so that he could kiss her and she was invaded by sensations from deep within her body. Her common sense warned her that it was madness to drift along in the mindless rapture he was awakening in her—and then she knew the delicious torture of trying to hold herself back when her body was screaming for him to love her. Although she hardly knew him, she felt she had known him all her life and she longed for him to tell her that he had fallen in love with her. She was also aware that he, in turn, was holding himself back, and then, after coaxing her to a point where she willingly parted her lips for him, she realised she was more than just a little prepared to go through the halting, uncertain stages of being made love to for the very first time. She felt, nevertheless, that there would be a point when she could resist him and be rational. Instead, the reverse was happening and she was unable to control the feelings which were surging through her entire body. What would happen afterwards she did not dare to think—and besides he had suggested marriage . . .

'You've bewitched me,' he murmured against her mouth. 'Not only have you succeeded in shaking up Holly's ideas, but you're also even getting me to change mine.'

Vaguely, Kristen was aware of a feeling of angry resentment, but she was too far gone to query his remark.

His hands went to her shoulders and then he began to fondle her breasts and the perfect buds of sensation there. He moved his hand down to her stomach where his fingers traced erotic patterns, moving across the crimson caftan and then down and up. Kristen found herself invaded by an almost terrifying desire, and when he moved over her and pushed his hands under her hips and lifted her up to him, his eyes impaled hers, searching and questioning. 'How do you take this thing off?' he asked, after a moment, referring to her caftan.

Their mouths were meeting again and previously unknown sensations surged through her, causing her to feel quite helpless, so that she made no attempt to take off her caftan and clung to him instead, hindering him.

His hands moved down her body and suddenly she thought—he's pushing me too far, and the spell, for her, was broken by fear.

'Nick,' she protested, pushing him away, 'don't! Don't do this to me. Why do you do these things to me?' Her voice rose.

'Why do you *let* me do them to you?' He spoke with shattering cruelty and she struggled to get away from him.

She gasped when he pushed her back on the sofa and followed the length of her body with his own, then suddenly, as if in self-disgust, he said, 'Forget it!'

After a moment she said, 'Why do I have this terrible feeling that I'm being punished for something, Nick?'

'I'm sorry.' He rolled away from her. 'If I'm punishing you, Kristen, I'm also punishing myself, believe me.'

She rose and hurriedly left him, and although she did not expect him to follow her, she locked the door to her room. She was shocked at the emotional earthquake he had caused within her, but this was the way she had known it would be, right from the moment she had heard his voice on the phone when he called from the airport.

CHAPTER FIVE

IT was still raining in the morning, but not as hard and not as slanting as it had been the day before. Kristen was up at six and, after staring out at the unrelenting high seas, she bathed and dressed, then went in search of Nick. She found him in the kitchen, making coffee.

As he looked up she said, 'I'll be leaving shortly.'

The air was charged with tension and then he replied, 'Well, if you want my opinion, I don't think you should leave.'

'I don't want your opinion. I don't need you to evaluate my ability to think for myself,' she retorted.

'Fine. You've certainly done okay, so far.' He shrugged indifferently. 'You'd better have something to eat before you go.'

'I'm not hungry. I'll have coffee, though.'

After a moment Kristen said, 'If I get through, shall I give Holly a message for you? Shall I let her know you're at the beach house?'

'There's no need for you to bow and scrape to Holly on my behalf,' he answered abruptly. 'She knows I can take care of myself. In any case, I didn't tell her I was coming here.'

'Yes, but don't you see, she might have been trying to phone you at your house or your office?'

Nick handed her a mug of coffee, and when he touched her she felt her senses jump. 'Kristen, just mind your own damned business and leave Holly to me, if you don't mind.' He lifted his own coffee mug and went to stand next to the door, where he leaned against the door-jamb, watching her with angry blue eyes.

She was wearing the black trousers with the white frilly blouse and the black jacket which went with both the trousers and the skirt. Her dark auburn hair fell to her shoulders and she was wearing golden-green earrings, the exact colour of her eyes. As usual, there was an air of sophistication about her.

On an impulse she said, 'All right I've been trying to understand you. I—give up!' She lifted one shoulder. 'You never say anything nice to me.'

'I wouldn't say that.' His deep blue eyes had a malicious glitter as he answered. 'I've often told you I think you're beautiful. I've told you I consider you to be desirable.'

'That's not what I mean, and you know it.' Kristen finished her coffee and put the mug down. Ridiculously, she wanted to cry. 'You've said some unforgivable things to me, Nick. You've done nothing but take your spite out on me. The feeling that exists between Holly and Barbro has nothing to do with me—in fact, I haven't even met Barbro. If you're going to allow your aunt to smash your engagement— well, that's your affair.'

'Holly may have the power to do a lot of things, but interfering in my engagement, or any relationship with *any* woman, for that matter, is not one of those things. I have no intention of allowing Holly to meddle in my private life.' His eyes dared her to argue, then he went on, 'I'll still be here, if you can't link up with the National Road and have to come back. If you do have to come back, I'll try very hard to say something nice.'

The hurt engulfed her. 'That's just the point—

you're so unfeeling. Everything you say to me is tinged with sarcasm. Anyway, it doesn't matter very much. Since you've fallen out with Holly I don't suppose we'll be seeing one another.'

'Don't count on it. There'll be many reasons for me to go back to the place of antiques, silver boxes and bowls of roses. The main reason is that Holly brought me up. She's like a mother to me. This isn't the first time we've had a row, and it won't be the last— unfortunately. These things happen. However, this row has sickened me and I feel as if I've lost my self-respect.'

Kristen was aware of the challenge in his eyes as he looked at her.

'And of course *I'm* to blame, right?' She turned away angrily. 'With you, hurt and sarcasm are ruling passions, and I think that goes for your fiancée as well. She seems to have gone out of her way to outrage poor Holly. I don't believe for a moment that Barbro and you might be splitting up. You just insinuated that to get me into bed with you. I'll see myself out.'

'I happen to be an exacting host. I'll see you to your car,' said Nick, but there was no sympathy in his handsome face, and she asked herself how she could have imagined herself to be in love with him.

On the way, under cover, to the carport she stood to look at the shattered syringa tree and felt she could easily identify with it.

Nick put her things into the car for her and stood back, his eyes resting on her. 'The rivers are down and the road's a mess. You should think, very seriously, about these things before you take off.'

'I *have* thought about them and I intend to make it—unless by this time the link road happens to have been washed away.' Kirsten's eyes were suddenly blurred by tears and she looked away quickly and stared at a magenta bougainvillaea which had collapsed beneath the weight of the rain.

Nick watched her as she slipped into the driver's seat, then, bending to look down at her, he said, 'Drive carefully.'

To hide the way she was feeling she said, 'I'll drive any way I choose—that is if this car starts. The rain has been lashing in here from all directions.

The Mazda started almost immediately, and with a quick glance at Nick, she reversed from the carport, turned in the area provided for this purpose and drove off. For a few moments it felt as if the car had left the driveway behind and had begun to float, and she caught a swift breath.

She was crying bitterly—unusual for her—but she allowed the tears to fall as she concentrated on driving. 'What the hell was all that in aid of?' she sobbed aloud. If anyone had told her that she would find Nick Lathbury at Salt Air and end up having a passionate love/hate relationship with him she would have laughed.

There were golden-yellow cannas growing in hollows on the side of the road. They were blurred by blinding pearl-grey rain and Kristen gave them a flickering glance. Through not concentrating properly, she hit a deep waterlogged pothole, after which she became more cautious and slackened to an almost crawling pace.

Because the bridge was under water, she had had to take a completely different route, going right out of her way in an effort to join up with the link road to the National Road. She had to drive slowly into the bargain, and thus, feeling utterly drained and exhausted, she arrived back at her flat towards evening.

Durban, she was told by Holly, had experienced heavy rain—the whiplash of the cyclone which had caused mountainous seas and terrific damage to the beach-front. Torrential rain and poor visiblity had caused many accidents, and damage to property and buildings was extensive.

'I've been so worried about you, dear,' Holly told her. 'I *knew* you'd gone up the North Coast, of course, and learned that it had been compltely cut off in a number of areas. Where did you stay? Not at Salt Air, by yourself, I hope?'

'No, Holly, not at Salt Air by myself. I managed. I was nervous, of course.' Kristen bit her lip and hoped Holly would not press for details. 'At this moment, I'm craving for a lovely bath and an early night. At least the rain isn't as heavy as it was.'

'Have dinner with me,' Holly invited. 'It will save you having to prepare something for yourself.'

'I'll be frank, Holly, all I feel like eating is a poached egg on toast—which I'll have in bed, I think.' Kristen forced herself to laugh lightly. In view of the fact that she was aware that Nick and Holly had quarrelled she felt self-conscious and unhappy.

'And I'll be perfectly honest with you, Kristen, I'm not very good company at the moment,' said Holly. 'You see, Nick and I had an awful row and I haven't seen him since. He's not at his town house and Lathbury Interiors know nothing. In any case, as it's the festive season, nothing much is happening there. All they know is that Nick said he wouldn't be in for a few days.'

Kristen listened helplessly. 'I'm sure he hasn't gone very far, Holly—maybe even to Salt Air. Who knows?'

'And there's no phone there,' Holly added. 'I feel very frustrated. I regard myself, with justification, as Nick's mother. We've had our differences, just as any mother and son would do, but we coped. We've always coped—until he met this girl. Perhaps he's cleared off with her . . . I don't know. She'd gone away, treacherous little cat, when she thought he wasn't going to be back for Christmas, but she might have come back—I just don't know.'

As she stood listening, Kristen felt like collapsing. 'I really must get out of these clothes,' she said. 'I'm feeling just too terrible.'

'Of course you must, and here I am holding you up. You look exhausted. I have a little gift for you, though, just to cheer you up. Just one moment . . .'

As Holly went off to get the gift Kristen stared after her in dismay. No wonder Nick was beginning to question what was going on, for there was the ring, the loan and storing of Holly's furniture, gifts of plants, a Flokati rug for Christmas and now this, whatever it was!

Holly came back carrying a potted plant. 'A pink pelargonium,' she said. 'Isn't it a beauty? I've been nursing it for weeks.'

Drowning in Holly's generosity, Kristen found herself stammering her thanks.

'And now, you go and have a lovely bath,' said Holly. Her mood seemed to have improved. 'Use a lot of bathsalts and put a little of the moisturising oil I gave you into the water. It's simply *marvellous*!'

Life, with Holly, Kristen thought, was back to normal.

*   *   *

The day Ferdi's airmail card arrived she was immediately tense. He had sent it to her office, and Kristen's hands were shaking as she opened it. 'Don't bother to meet my plane,' he had written. He had, however, given her the date of his departure from Heathrow which would give her the information, after checking, concerning his arrival in South Africa. He had signed the card—Ferdi. Just Ferdi. He had also mentioned that he had something to tell her and would be in touch. Staring at the card, Kristen thought bitterly, I'll write a bestseller and call it *Just Ferdi*.

She made up her mind to meet the plane, however. She also made up her mind to forget about Nicholas Lathbury.

Wearing a pale willow-green cotton suit, she was at the airport twenty minutes before Ferdi's plane touched down, and a short while later her eyes were scanning the passengers as they came straggling through to the arrivals lounge.

Ferdi was with a very young girl who had long curly blonde hair, almost frizzy, and a small childlike face. She was wearing khaki trousers and a fawn cashmere sweater beneath a terracotta trench-coat, for after all, she had come from a wintry climate. Heavy gold bracelets glistened and clanked, no doubt, on both fragile wrists. Next to the tall, dark Ferdi she appeared delicate and so much younger. Ferdi, Kristen thought, had obviously sat next to this young woman on the plane and had been helping her wherever possible.

All at once he turned his head, and as their eyes met, Kristen was aware of his shock and she half-lifted her arm to wave, then dropped it and went on watching as he started to push the trolley again. There was only the one trolley between them and, clutching a travel handbag, the girl walked by his side.

Directly they drew level with Kristen, Ferdi said, 'I didn't expect you. Didn't you get my card?' His voice sounded angry.

'I did get your card.' Kristen was aware of the girl's suddenly hostile eyes. 'Yes, I did,' she said again, 'but I didn't think you meant it.' She regarded him with distrust.

While they stood crushed together in a mass of people pushing trolleys, he said, 'Kristen, this is Reba. We met in Gstaad. I'll be frank—we're ... living together.'

Kristen tried to get her mind to adjust to the position she found herself in, then she said, 'I see.' She spoke in the carefully modulated voice she used when doing business with important clients. 'Well,' she took a little breath and released it quickly, 'you won't want to be reminded that you were engaged to me, will you? So I'll leave you to—er—live together. On the other hand, I don't wish to be reminded that I was ever engaged to you, so,' she took off her engagement ring and handed it to him, 'here's your ring. Maybe you'll be able to trade it in for something a little—well, younger looking.'

For a moment Ferdi looked blank, then he took the ring from her and slipped in into his pocket.

'I wanted to explain in private,' he was saying, 'but you didn't give me the chance, so you can hardly blame me for having to do it this way, can you?'

'Don't bother to explain,' her voice, now, was like a chill wind, 'or you might just hear something you don't particularly want to. There are worse things in life than being discarded by you, believe me.'

Ferdi received this piece of news in silence, and then, without looking at the girl, Kristen turned and made her way towards the entrance of the building. The shock she was feeling had almost a physical weight about it—and yet, mingled with this shock, she felt a sense of relief.

The Mazda was hot from the sun and the moment she got into it she rolled down the window and took a long breath, then, starting the car, she drove into town and, after parking it at the office block, went straight to her office on the eighteenth floor, where she was blessed with a breathtaking view of the Bay. Going to an ornate mirror on one wall, she methodically checked her make-up, then, with a shaking hand, applied a new coral lipstick.

The very last thing she felt like was work, but for the next three hours, she forced herself to concentrate on it. From time to time she glanced down at the space where Ferdi's ring had once glistened, sparkled and glittered, and felt an impotent fury. Outwardly calm, however, she appeared remote and businesslike.

This was one day in her life when she wished she had work out of town, work which entailed hour after hour of driving. Her office, with its baskets of growing greenery, white wicker sofa and chairs, upholstered in lime-green and coral-pink, held no appeal. The telephones, olive-green and white, got on her nerves with their petulant chirping. A white and gold showcase, the length of one wall, displayed opulent gold-rimmed jars and flagons, a reminder that her life was supposed to revolve around glamour.

So much seemed to have happened to her, and it was incredible to think that it was still the festive season. For a few moments she toyed with the idea of taking time off and catching a flight to Cape Town so that she could, at least, bring in the New Year with Craig and Libby, but this was before the postal delivery and subsequent discovery of a letter from Libby. In her letter Libby conveyed all good wishes for the forthcoming New Year and passed on the exciting news that she and Craig had been invited to bring in the New Year on board a yacht belonging to a friend.

So that took care of that.

The following day she was on the road again, even though it was New Year's Eve. It was a trip in the direction of the mountains and could be made in one day unless there happened to be a calamity. Once again her emergency overnight bag contained fresh undies and sleepwear and all the items Kristen might need if she had to spend the night away from home for some unexpected reason. Her attaché case was filled with vials, small and large ornate bottles and jars, blown-up photographs, advertisements and even a folder of the most beautiful publicity stills, which she had been responsible for organising.

Everything worked out with the precision of a computer and she was on her way home with time to breathe. Her whole body seemed to be one big ache, all she could think of was a warm, fragrant bath—and bed.

She had no sooner parked her car than she noticed Nick's dark green Jaguar which was parked in Holly's driveway. He was about to get into it when he noticed Kristen and, instead came over to where she was getting her things out of the Mazda.

'Here let me help you,' he said.

'I can manage myself, thank you.' Her voice was cool.

'I want to talk to you,' he said.

'I have nothing to say to you, Nick, and now will you please——'

'Why don't you want to talk to me?' he cut in.

'You should know why.' She swung round on him. 'That's a stupid question, isn't it? I'm also deeply distrustful of you. As it happens, I'm deeply distrustful of all men—now get out of my way!'

'By the way, I've heard about your broken engagement,' he said easily.

'Holly's been busy,' she said sarcastically. 'So you've made it up?'

'We've made it up, yes, but that doesn't mean I approve of a lot of things.'

'Well, I have no answer to that,' she said, and suddenly she felt out of control and realised she was tired, depressed and fed-up with the whole business. She was wearing jeans and a dusky-blue shirt with a navy scarf tucked into the neck and a pair of huge sunglasses framed her face, and pushing them to the top of her head, she said, 'I can manage my own luggage.'

'I know you can, but I'm going to manage it for you,' Nick said curtly.

The sun, preparing to set, was sparking fire to a bank of clouds and Holly's garden was ablaze with hibiscus and bougainvillaea which had managed to outsmart the whiplash of the cyclone.

'Oh, damn you!' she snapped. 'Anyway, give me that attaché case—I'd hate you to drop it.'

'Like Ferdi dropped you?' His handsome face was inscrutable.

Furious with him, she said, 'It didn't quite turn out that way. *I* gave the ring back.'

They had reached the door to her entrance hall and she turned to look at him. 'Well, my day has been a long and a busy one and I want to simmer down. If you leave my case on the doorstep, I'll carry it inside myself.'

'Meaning, of course, that you have no intention of inviting me in?' He was wearing a very light yellow cashmere jersey and cotton jeans.

'Meaning just that, yes.' Kristen gave him a frustrated look. 'Nick, why don't you just go and crawl under a rock?'

'I want to tell you I've been giving prolonged thought to a certain silk-flower-massed house,' he said, 'and I'll be honest with you—I missed you, after you left.' He grinned. 'I nearly took the flaunting cactus to bed, just to feel near you.'

'How very touching!' She took a long breath and then went on, 'Nick, I consider what took place between us at Salt Air was ridiculous. I guess the cyclone went to my head. I mean, think of it—all that whirling, rotating wind was enough to drive anyone mad! But, like a cyclone, it had a limited diameter—a limited measurement——'

He cut in, 'But of magnifying *power*, right? Increasing power.' He laughed softly. 'There's something surprisingly naïve about you, Kristen, for all your big ideas in life and your surprising knowledge of what makes a cyclone tick.'

'What I'm trying to say, Nick, is . . . what happened at Salt Air was just one of those things.'

'It *did* cause widespread havoc, though.' His blue eyes were mocking. 'Am I right?'

'Perhaps . . . but it went whirling and rotating until it blew itself out—which is what happened in our case.'

She began searching for her key and, when she had found it, she said, 'Furthermore, I don't want anything to do with you. I haven't forgotten some of the things you said to me, éven if you have.'

'Aren't you going to invite me in?' he asked. 'I was hoping you would offer me a drink. After all, it does happen to be New Year's Eve.'

'And Barbro's still away,' she added spitefully.

'And you've had your chips with Ferdi,' he answered, just as spitefully.

Recognising the attraction he always held for her, she sighed, 'Oh, all right, come in, for heaven's sake.'

When she had poured him a drink and a tomato juice cocktail for herself she said, 'You might as well know it—I'm tired. I'm irritable and I don't like you very much—so—drink your drink and go.'

With considerable mockery he said, 'You mustn't give in to fatigue when you're going out.'

'I'm not going out,' she answered.

'I want you to come out with me.'

'I'm not interested in going out with you—besides, where do you think you'd go at this late hour?' It was ridiculous to feel excited, she thought, and her golden-green eyes brooded on his face.

'I'll make a plan. Leave it to me.' She watched him as he got up and poured himself another drink and then added the ice which she had brought from the kitchen.

'I don't remember offering you another drink.' She gave him a long look. 'Actually, I'm waiting for you to leave.'

'What are you doing tonight?' he asked, running his finger-tip round the rim of the glass and looking back at her.

'I'm having a luxurious bath, something to eat, and then I'm going to bed with a nice book.'

'You intend bringing in the New Year with a book?' Nick looked amused.

'Yes.' She blinked. 'I'm on a book kick, actually.'

He took a sip of his drink. 'What's the title of this book?'

Kristen thought for a moment, then she said, 'Is it important?'

'Very important.'

'Well, if you must know, it's called *Lays of Ancient Rome* by Lord Macaulay.'

Nick laughed outright and she discovered, with a little thrill, that he had an attractive rich laugh, and she loved him for it. 'You must be joking,' he said.

'I'm not.' She bit her lip, then said, 'I'll show you, if you like.'

'Kristen, you can put going to bed with *Lays of Ancient Rome* out of your mind.' He raised his glass halfway to his lips, then put it down and came over to where she was standing. 'All day you've had nothing but hassles, haven't you?' He was very close to her and she tried to keep her eyes from going to his mouth, so she lifted her lashes and gazed right into his eyes. Feeling the power of them, she looked away.

'Okay.' She tried to keep her voice flippant. 'So—all day, I've had nothing but hassles.'

'And you're in one hell of a rat-race, right?'

'And you have this tremendous gift of uplifting one, don't you?' Her voice was abrupt. 'Yes, I am in a rat-race. Who isn't, these days? Think of all the pop stars. They're on a crest of the wave one moment and dumped—stranded on the beach—the next. But they've got to keep working at it, make a comeback.

Are you trying to tell me that my being in a rat-race is an excuse for going out with you?'

'Yes, that is just what I'm telling you. While you're having that luxurious bath and making yourself beautiful I'm going back to my Spanish hacienda type house and I'm going to arrange a booking somewhere, then plump up the cushions in my living-room—for afterwards. I'll ring you, just as soon as I can, to let you know where this night-spot will be. Wherever it is, we'll dine, wine and dance, and I hope we'll take in a cabaret. What have you got to say?'

Kristen looked away and then back at him and, on a fluttery little breath, she said, 'Very well, I'll go with you—and I'll kick myself later.'

He left her feeling confused and angry with herself for having said she would go out with him, and when he phoned her thirty minutes later, her voice was stilted as she answered.

'I've managed to book a table at the Scarlet Ibis,' he told her. 'Do you know it?'

Did she know it? If her voice had been stilted before, it was crippled now as her thoughts immediately flew to Ferdi. Why did Nick have to arrange a booking at the very place where she and Ferdi had celebrated their engagement? After all, they had been very much in love and very happy. She glanced down at her finger, which suddenly looked very naked—the lighter shade of the skin a dismal reminder of their love.

Nick was saying something, and she shook her hair back and looked up.

'What did you say?' she asked.

'I said—dinner, dancing and cabaret ... special singing star, or something.'

'Well, fine, I'd like that.' As she glanced down again, her naked finger mocked her.

'Good. I'll pick you up at seven-thirty.' She could almost see his brief smile—the groove in one cheek.

While she was in the bath, she considered what to wear and decided on a dress which she had not yet worn. It was a dress created in Florence, and made of such soft material that it could fit into a tiny packet almost without creasing. She had bought it with an island honeymoon in mind. It was black and patterned with apricot and deep pink-tinged hibiscus blooms. With it, she decided to wear her black, high-heeled sandals, earrings of beaten gold and a gold bracelet.

It was a cool, perfect night for dining and dancing and, because they were going to the Scarlet Ibis, a perfect reminder of Ferdi.

There was an exciting festive air about the night-spot, which was part of the magnificent Gabrielle Hotel on the North Coast. The room was perfectly air-chilled and the lighting kind to women and flowers alike. Waiters stood around in scarlet jackets and black trousers while silver, crystal and porcelain glittered and gleamed beneath soft table-lighting and there was a sophisticated profusion of overhead Christmas decorations.

As they were being shown to the small round table, with its white-skirted cloth dropping to the carpet, Kristen tried not to look at the shiny space which was the dance floor and where she and Ferdi had danced on that particular romantic occasion of her life.

At this stage of the night, the live quartet was playing strictly relaxed dining music and, vaguely, she answered Nick's question as to what she would like to drink before they decided to go through to the buffet tables which awaited guests.

From the table, which was next to a long sweep of glass, there was a spectacular vista of the coastline where the scattered lights became more and more concentrated until they centred on Durban, which was situated on a curve and sheltered by the Bluff. Immediately in front of the hotel the illuminated swimming-pool created more drama and, beyond that, the translucent surf rolled in before thumping down on the pale sweep of beach.

The chairs around all the tables were hip-hugging, like space-age chairs, but covered in pale gold raw silk, and, trying to obliterate the memories which began to take over, Kristen fidgeted about in hers. Across the room, a wall covered with rose-tinted mirrors emphasised the expanse of the dining-room and she could just make out their table and her own miserable face—for she had decided to be miserable. My life is a mess, she found herself thinking bitterly.

'Cheer up!' Nick's sarcastic voice broke into her restless thoughts. 'I'm not absolutely sure why you're so broken up over this man, but, according to Holly, you're well rid of him.' His low laugh was tantalising.

In a controlled state of fury she retorted, 'How does Holly know I'm well rid of him? She hardly knows him. Why did you have to bring up the subject of Ferdi? Have you no feelings? How would *you* like it if I started on Barbro who, by rights, should be here with you?'

He leaned back and regarded her with something like mockery. 'Right now, Barbro happens to be a smudge on the horizon,' he told her. 'I'm more concerned with the present—and what it has to offer.

The future? Well,' he lifted his shoulders, 'time will tell, won't it?'

'That's intelligent, isn't it? Any fool knows that.' Kristen's voice was sneering.

People were beginning to leave their tables to go and serve themselves at the long, scarlet-clothed buffet tables which were reached by going through wide glass doors and crossing the pink marble floor of a flower and plant-filled foyer, where clusters of bronze and silver coloured balloons floated from an ornate cream and gold ceiling. The sweeping stairway to the ground floor trailed greenery and flowers from behind intricately scrolled wrought-iron work. The foyer was also treated as an exhibition place for a collection of contemporary paintings—all of flowers, enough to fill a field, and, seeing them, Kristen immediately thought of the paintings at Salt Air. There were paintings of petunias and roses, pale yellow daisies and wild lilies, purple and yellow irises and pictures of birds and roses.

'The girl who painted these specialises in flowers and birds,' Nick was saying. 'She has a gallery around the corner from here. At one time, I think I must have bought her entire collection—I know the gallery was left standing bare. You must have noticed them at the beach house?'

'I did.' Kristen felt a prickle of jealousy at the mention of this girl. 'You bought them for Holly, you mean?'

'I bought them for myself,' he answered carelessly, and the groove in his cheek deepened. 'I bought them—well, because her style is really very unusual and because I also happen to be very fond of her.'

'Who is this girl?' She stopped walking so that she

could peer at the signature of one of the paintings. 'Is she Barbro?'

'Her name is Nicola,' he said.

'Nicola and Nicholas.' She found she was jealous. 'You seem to get around. Tell me, have you asked her to marry you, too?'

He laughed softly. 'Since she already happens to be married, I didn't want to interrupt anything.'

'I didn't think you had it in you,' she answered spitefully. 'Such gallantry!'

'You sound jealous,' he said.

'Huh!' She turned away and began walking away from him.

Scarlet-coated waiters fussed over them as they helped themselves to food from tables displaying a mouth-watering assortment of hot and cold food, beneath shivering, glittering and expensive decorations.

By the time they got back to their table, Kristen's mood had lifted slightly and she said, 'I'll get fat on all this delicious food. Did you notice the super desserts?' She was suddenly determined to conquer her depression.

For a moment, Nick's blue eyes rested on her bosom, then he said, 'I can't imagine you getting fat. Even when you're an old, old lady, you'll still look good.'

'Really?' She picked up her scarlet table napkin with slender fingers which were topped by fingernails like pink sugared almonds. Lifting her lashes so that she could look at him, she said, 'But you still don't like me, do you?'

'Do you want me to like you? Is it important?'

Lifting one shoulder, she said, 'It's no big deal, actually. I don't really care.' She began to eat.

After a few moments he said, 'Tell me, what did you do today?'

Without looking up she said, 'Oh ... I worked. What do you think I did? You know about my work for House of Marini. Well, today,' she stopped eating and glanced at him, 'I was taken on a tour of a cosmetic factory. It really was very interesting.'

'Tell me about it.'

'Are you really interested?' There was an edge to her voice.

'Sure, I'm interested.'

'I watched a new and exciting lipstick being creamed in huge, huge vats. It was fantastic and quite odd. You see, I kept wishing I could eat some of it. The vats were swirling with rich, pink cream.' She laughed lightly. 'It looked good enough to eat!' Thawing out with him, she continued, 'This is all part of my training—I have to know what I'm selling. Afterwards, I was treated to a very swish lunch. This is also part of my life. Quite exciting, actually, so long as you don't end up in a state of complete exhaustion.'

Sitting opposite her, Nick was immaculately tailored and handsome. His eyes, she was thinking, might be dark blue with thick black lashes, but they were undeniably and demandingly masculine. He caught her gaze and held it.

'Where did you eat this—very swish lunch?' he asked.

'In an executive dining-room in the Capital,' she laughed a little. 'Along with a lot of distinguished-looking men with big expense accounts.'

His eyes went on regarding her with speculative interest from across the dimly lit table. 'And so you were the focal point?' He was plainly disappointed to hear that she had lunched with men.

'Yes, you could say that. After all, I was the only female there. I felt attractive and completely in control.' She gave him a long look, then lifted her wine glass and touched it to her lips. Afterwards, she added, 'It's not often that I'm out of control, Nicholas.'

He gave her a long look. 'We must pursue that again, some time,' he said.

They continued to eat in silence and Kristen listened vaguely to the music, which was still romantic.

After a few moments he said, 'What you were trying to say just now is that you were not in control at Salt Air. In fact, you were out of control on several occasions, if I remember correctly—which I'm sure I do.'

'Yes, I was.' She felt a sudden rush of excitement. 'I had no idea you'd be there when I turned up at Salt Air, believe it or not. You, of course, thought I'd tracked you down.' She gave him a wide, angry stare.

'Let's just forget what I thought. Tell me, where do you stay on those other occasions when you can't make the journey in one day? I'm not referring to the North Coast now.'

'Oh,' her shrug was careless, for the wine was leaving her feeling very successful all of a sudden, 'sometimes I manage to book into a three or four-star hotel where, again, a large number of guests are mainly businessmen passing through. Travelling the way I do, I often find myself in a man's world.'

'What makes you say it's a man's world?' He sounded impatient.

'Well, you just have to take a look round some of the dining-rooms, or a glimpse into the dimly lit cocktail bars, to see all the male reps there. In a way, it's sad to see them. Most of them look so bored and fed-up on their same old bar-stools and twirling their glasses round and round on the same old counters they'd sat at—perhaps a week or two before. You hardly ever see a woman rep, by the way, although it's getting to be more frequent.'

'And so you're a very successful female rep with an Italian leather and gold-leaf-initialled attaché case and an expense account?' He looked at her with faint amusement.

'I do have an expense account, yes. After all, sometimes I have to lunch with manufacturers and buyers.' She took a ruffled little breath. 'You don't have to be sarcastic.'

Ignoring her remark, he said, 'At least you don't have an expense account figure like some of your cronies.'

'Nick,' she felt furious, 'the days of taunting women are over. See? Don't ask me about my lifestyle just to poke fun at me.'

People were beginning to dance when they were not helping themselves from the buffet tables across the pink marble-floored foyer and the music was being pepped up.

'Would you like to dance?' asked Nick.

'Yes, I'd like that,' she answered, considering the fact that it was New Year's Eve, after all. As she stood up she felt herself begining to float hazily, and this concerned her because she was not in the habit of drinking as much as she had been doing since the beginning of the festive season.

Women, she noticed a little angrily, seemed to go out of their way to look at Nick. The tempo of the music had changed again and they found themselves dancing to the kind of Glenn Miller music that her mother must have danced to when she was young. It was slow and slinky dance music and aimed to please all ages at this time of the year—when a new one was just around the corner.

As he drew her closer Nick's chin brushed her hair and she could feel his body, warm and hard, moving against her own, and beneath the flimsy layered gown, she was aware of the flame of desire that leapt upwards, almost engulfing her.

'What are you thinking about?' he asked, breaking into her thoughts and holding her away from him so that he could look into her eyes. She felt his irritation and realised that he was probably thinking she had been brooding about Ferdi.

Staring wide-eyed back at him, she said, 'I was listening to the music.'

'Like hell you were!'

'Okay . . . I was thinking of my mother.'

'And you expect me to believe that? Telling the truth is obviously not your strong point, Miss Ashton.'

'I don't have to defend myself.' Her voice was huffy.

'I brought you here to enjoy yourself,' he went on. 'I didn't bring you here to re-live old times and brood about your ex.'

'Let's face it,' she retorted, 'you brought me here to amuse yourself—to take your mind off Miss Barbro— or perhaps even the married Nicola?'

The music ended and they went back to their table.

'Do you have to make it so bloody obvious that

you're so shattered by events?' Nick went on. 'Do me a favour, don't burden me with your jangling Gstaad problems.' He took her arm. 'No, don't sit down. Let's go and get something more to eat.'

Beside him, Kristen walked with the grace of an angry leopard, her breasts emphasised by the layered black, hibiscus-strewn dress which started to layer downwards from immediately below pencil-slim shoulder straps. As she went ahead of him, his moody eyes followed her movements with impatient interest.

As they helped themselves to roast wild duck, deliciously white turkey and pink beef, he said, 'By the way, I like your dress.' His voice, for once, was almost gentle.

She did not look at him. 'Thank you. It cost a lot of money.'

'Does everything with you have to revolve around money?' He spoke in a loud voice, and they both looked round to see whether they were attracting attention.

Very softly she said, 'And what do I take *that* to mean? All I said was——'

'I know what you said.' There was a rasp of impatience in his voice.

'It *should* be a lovely dress,' she went on, and stopped serving herself to give him an angry look. 'I paid more than I like to think for it. Is there anything wrong in that? What's more, I paid for it myself. Having you talk like this is sickening—just as it was at Salt Air when you did nothing but sling off and pass snide remarks.'

People were beginning to walk round them now, trying not to notice the feud taking place. There were discreet smiles.

When they got back to their table a girl with a husky Italian voice was singing that old favourite—'Smile When Your Heart Is Breaking'.

Well, that had to come, Kristen thought, deciding that Ferdi had broken her heart.

The girl was dark and sensually beautiful and her rounded breasts moved beneath the crimson dress she was wearing. Glancing at Nick, Kristen saw that his blue eyes brooded on them, and she suddenly felt let down and abused.

'I feel thoroughly miserable,' she said, childishly voicing her feelings.

Looking at her, he said, 'I can't hear you. Why don't you save it until the cabaret is over?' His eyes went back to the girl and, very deliberately, they moved slowly over her entire body while Kristen watched, seething.

Immediately the cabaret was over people began to unwind and ate, talked, laughed and danced with typical festivity abandon, with the promise of the birth of a wonderful and peaceful New Year, not very far off. Soon there was to be a new year, and it was unthinkable to Kristen that she was in love with the uncaring Nicholas Lathbury. He was the man who had sent urgent, aching sensations through her entire body at a beach house called Salt Air, where silk flowers sprouted from an assortment of baskets and vases. Suddenly, she was invaded by misery, and although something told her that it was the way in which she was reacting to having had too much wine, she could not help feeling sorry for herself.

'What were you saying during the cabaret?' asked Nick.

'Nothing.' Her face was sullen, like a child's.

'You said you were feeling thoroughly miserable.'

'Then why did you ask?' she snapped.

'Stop being childish, Kristen!' There was anger in his voice.

'I *feel* childish, Nicholas.'

'Why do you feel miserable?' He put his elbow on the table and put his chin in the palm of his hand and went on looking at her.

'Do you know something?' Her voice was bitter. 'I've never even had the experience of being on a yacht with a man.'

'And that's why you're feeling unhappy?'

'You had the damn cheek to say that I turned up at Salt Air like a flaunting cactus—that I'd come there to flaunt myself . . .'

'And yet you've never had the experience of being on a yacht with a man. Alone with a man, you mean?' He took his elbow off the table and sat back and regarded her.

'Yes. *Alone* with a man.'

'Did you want to go away with a man—on a yacht, that is?'

'No, I didn't *want* to—but I'm beginning to wish now that the opportunity had presented itself.'

'In other words, you regret not having been on a yacht orgy?' His expression was one of anger. 'A period at sea of wild dancing, drinking, singing—and debauchery. Right?' He released an impatient breath. 'Look,' he said, 'you may have an Italian leather attaché case and an expense account, but that doesn't change the fact that you're a little fool. Come and dance, before I say too much.' He got up and, coming round to her, reached for her hand.

They danced to 'I Love You Just The Way You

Are', and Nick held her very close. 'That goes for me, too,' he said, against her cheek. 'Like my eccentric aunt, I've fallen for you.'

'I don't know how anybody could love you,' she retorted, loving him.

About a minute to midnight he said, 'What are your New Year resolutions, Miss Ashton?' She could feel his warm breath against her cheek.

'I intend, like your eccentric aunt, not to trust men and to live my life out as a spinster.' Suddenly she laughed and a little devil prompted her to say, 'A generous spinster.' She was thinking a little furiously— yes, Holly, you got me into this, with your ring and your potted plants, not to mention your Flokati rug and the 'on loan' furniture.

'That sounds more like you.' Nick's voice was hard. 'What about the yacht trip? What would he have been like—this man with a yacht?'

'Oh,' she lifted her slim shoulders, 'rich.' Because of the music and babble of voices she had to lift her voice. 'Very rich, with a cruel, mobile face.'

'And a mobile bank account, of course,' Nick cut in.

'Of course. I mentioned that first—or words to that effect. He would have a bold stare, from greenish eyes. He would be lean, hard, learned, sophisticated, middle-aged with coarse, curly hair, going silver.' Kristen was caught up in the fun. 'And you—what are your resolutions?'

'One—not to underestimate the devious ways of women, and two—to propose to one of them, anyway.'

It was midnight, and he crushed her to him fiercely and kissed her with a violence that frightened her. Pushed and shoved about by revellers, they clung together, and the feel of him excited her so much that, of her own accord, she parted her lips under his. When he drew back he said, 'Marry me, Kristen—to hell with everybody and everything.'

'You don't mean it,' she said.

'I do.' His mouth bit into hers again. 'That's the way it's got to be.'

'You don't even love me,' she said, as they broke apart, then gasped as Nick almost swung her away from a man and a girl who were blowing whistles made of paper which shot out like the tongues of attacking reptiles, into their faces.

'I love you enough,' he said. 'Come—we're going back to my place.'

'No,' she said. 'No.'

'Yes,' he answered. 'Yes. This isn't the tenth century.'

CHAPTER SIX

NICK was waiting for a break in the traffic as, one by one, the cars left the hotel grounds. Somebody had released a huge cluster of balloons which floated past the dark green Jaguar.

'Everybody is very happy.' Kristen's voice sounded young and lonely.

He turned impatiently. 'Aren't you?'

'No, I'm not.'

Nick concentrated on getting out of the traffic snarl, then he said, 'Try to be—if it's not too much trouble.'

She knew she should demand to be taken straight to her flat, but remained silent. What are you doing to yourself? she wondered despairingly. Nick treated her as he would some criminal, and yet she was attracted to him sexually and was sure she was in love with him.

'What's the the problem?' he asked, through the darkness.

'I don't want to talk,' she answered shortly. 'Just leave me alone.'

Some time later he said, 'We're nearly there. Are you tired?'

'Yes,' she answered, in a tight voice, 'I am.'

While her eyes brooded into the night he went on, 'There's a wonderful view of the lights from my house. I think you'll like it.' When she made no reply he said, 'There's a palm tree, which reflects into the pool and a huge hibiscus shrub, and sometimes hibiscus blooms float in the water.'

'Really?' Kristen's voice was off-hand.

The car was climbing the steep drive now, leading to the town houses which curved round a hill.

'Apparently,' Nick was saying, 'the builders were very particular about preserving all trees on the site. Usually they're hacked down without any thought.'

'I know. It happens all the time,' she answered, but her mind wasn't on trees. She was thinking of Nick's proposal of marriage and about what she was doing to herself by coming here.

The town house was at the top of a long drive and resembled a huge, sprawling Spanish hacienda, with walls that gleamed white in the night beneath a red-tiled roof. The arched windows and balconies were designed to command the view of Durban and the distant coast-line, and Kristen noticed several ships, awaiting entry to the harbour, anchored out at sea, their lights glimmering on the water.

Nick turned into the private driveway which led to the courtyard and, a few moments later, she stood beside him as he unlocked and opened huge double doors of carved and brass-studded wood. Unsure of herself and of him, she hesitated before she followed him into the hall. When he had turned on a light he moved to one side for her to pass.

The view from the lounge was certainly impressive, and she was amazed at the sense of space created by the white plaster walls, dark beams, and the unusual and successful combination of colours which she took in at a sweeping glance—acid-yellow and lime-green, with the occasional injection of bright pink. Two large sofas were covered in white canvas and crowded with cushions of these colours. There were two acid-green chairs and the carpet was off-white pure wool. An

Italian cupboard housed drinks and a low carved antique chest looked as if it might have come from Holly's house because it was obviously a family heirloom like the Italian cupboard. A dark-pink pottery bowl, filled with peaches, stood on the huge glass-topped coffee table which stood on legs of gleaming brass. There were books, with colourful jackets, on low tables and beautiful lamps. Her eyes rested on a metal wall bracket light and Nick said casually, 'Art Nouveau.'

There were no pictures, but instead, one huge and truly magnificent tapestry, and there were fresh flowers.

'What do you think of it?' asked Nick, on his way to the Italian drinks cupboard.

'Mmm . . . fresh flowers,' she said, laughing lightly.

'Uh-huh, especially for you.' He turned to look at her.

'Do you expect me to believe that? You weren't even sure if I'd come here.'

'I banked on it—but tell me, what do you think of this room?'

'It's beautiful,' Kristen answered honestly, her golden-green eyes sweeping here and there. 'It's not at all ultra-masculine, and yet it has a sophistication which makes it a very acceptable—and expected— place for man to live in. It's vibrant—more than beautiful, actually.' Thinking of the Prentice home where Barbro had used her talents as a designer, she felt a spurt of jealousy. 'Did—Barbro have a hand in it?'

'No, she didn't.' There was an edge to his voice. 'Would you say it's a place for seduction?' He stopped pouring drinks to give her a mocking glance.

'I didn't come here to be seduced,' she answered quickly, but she had, just previous to his remark, begun to be aware that he was thinking of making love to her, and this made her excited but cautious.

'There's a spacious bedroom and a long balcony that looks down on the pool and across the lights of town and the sea in the distance. Shall we take our drinks up there?' She was aware of the mockery in his eyes, but he sounded tense. She knew he was feeling his way with her.

'No!' she answered angrily, then watched him as he put on some relaxing music. When he took off his jacket and began to undo his tie she felt her breath beginning to come with difficulty. Her eyes brooded on his fingers as he undid his shirt and she could not stop her gaze from going over him.

The air-conditioner hummed quietly, yet he said, 'I'm hot. Do you feel hot?'

'No.' She took a ruffled little breath.

Wide-eyed and nervous, she watched him as he shrugged out of his shirt and tossed it on to a nearby chair to join his jacket and his tie.

'There's no need to strip down,' she said. 'If you think you're being wildly attractive, Nicholas, you have another think coming.'

She was aware of his deep blue eyes on her, mocking and challenging. 'You're bad news, Kristen. Do you know that?'

'Why am I bad news?'

'Because no matter how much I've tried not to think about you, I don't succeed.'

'I'm beginning to feel decidedly angry,' she told him. 'This is a ridiculous way to spend the evening . . . I mean, it's a ridiculous way to *end* the evening, and I'd like to go now. After all, it's terribly late.'

Her mind was whirling from having had too much to drink and she tried to concentrate on the view, which was amazing enough, on its own, to stir the senses, never mind being with the music and Nick's tanned torso, which was covered with dark, glistening hairs.

'I've had too much wine and champagne to drink this,' she said, as he placed a glass in front of her. 'I feel awful. I'm not going to drink it, whatever it is. I'm not really used to drinking.'

He came round to where she was settled among the green and dark pink cushions and reached for her hand.

'In that case, come and get some fresh air. It will clear your head—and mine too, for that matter.'

'Where?' she asked quickly, thinking of the upstairs balcony.

'To the poolside. I'll pick you a hibiscus bloom and you can tuck it into your hair. It will match the hibiscus flowers on your dress.'

'Oh, must I?' Kristen was laughing, suddenly, and felt too languid to stand up. 'Really, I'm quite comfortable here.'

Nick bent down and almost lifted her from the sofa, and when she was standing next to him his eyes dropped to her mouth. Bewitched by the music, she felt a wave of sensual pleasure; she swayed towards him and his arms closed about her. The feel of his warm, hairy chest was overwhelming, and then his lips sought hers and she closed her eyes. Her arms went to his back and she thrilled at the warmth of his skin. There was not a scrap of unwanted weight on him, and she found herself stroking his back and then dragging her oval finger-nails across it.

'I need you so much,' he said against her mouth, and pressing his thighs against hers. He parted her lips and she responded immediately.

After a moment, she came to her senses and pulled away from him. 'Nick, this is nonsense! If you want to show me your pool—well, okay, show it to me, and then take me home.'

'Come on, then.' There was impatience in his voice.

'What about your shirt?' she asked.

'To hell with my shirt. What do I want a shirt for?'

'The neighbours might see you. I mean, this is a town house, after all, not some secluded country mansion in the foothills.'

'I don't think this is the favourite time of morning for neighbours to be interested in what's going on in my garden,' Nick answered impatiently, and began to lead her in the direction of the sun-room, which had three long and shallow steps, directly off the lounge. The sun-room was painted a shocking but very pleasing pink, and the floor was covered with pale honey-coloured tiles which extended through sliding glass doors to the pool area. White furniture was cushioned in parrot-green and scattered with pink and emerald-green pillows, and Kristen knew that during the day these colours, as they mingled with the blue water of the pool, would be absolutely stunning.

The pool area was not large and it was walled in, to make it private. It was big enough, however, for a patch of emerald-green lawn and the exotic palm tree which could be seen from the foot of the drive leading up to the houses. Nearby, a hibiscus shrub was a cascade of giant pink blooms, their huge, frilly petals open to the night.

Kristen's spirits were immediately uplifted. 'Oh,

how gorgeous,' she said, and watched as Nick went to pluck one of the flowers. When he came back to her he said, 'It's called Southern Belle. She's a big, floppy girl, as you can see, but a very lovely one.' As he tucked in into her hair he added, 'It's so perfect it could easily be mistaken for one of your silk flowers.'

Growing in tubs nearby, the exotic leaves of plants swayed about in the wind which caught at the fragile hibiscus-strewn material of Kristen's dress and blew it about her legs.

Nick's hands dropped from her hair to her hips and, as he pulled her towards him, she felt a wave of excitement wash over her.

'This isn't fair,' she said, after a moment.

'Why isn't it fair?' He looked into her eyes.

'You brought me here to make love to me, didn't you?' She spoke carefully, spacing her words. 'Well, didn't you?' Her voice was accusing.

'I've also asked you to marry me,' he said, very softly.

'Oh, great! But you didn't say *why* you asked me to marry you—that is, if you still intend to keep your promise after you've had sex on the rocks.'

Kissing her fingertips, he said, 'Isn't having asked you to marry me enough? I want to marry you—very much.'

When he picked her up she gasped and then began laughing. 'Nick, if you drop me into this pool, I'll never forgive you! I told you, this gown cost a small fortune.'

She closed her eyes and then opened them again as he carried her round the pool and then back into the sun-room and through to the lounge. Her head was swimming and everything she saw was a confusion of glowing lights and colour.

Nick virtually dropped her on to one of the sofas, then lifted her feet off the carpet and began to take off her black, high-heeled sandals.

'I don't think this is a very good idea,' she said, trying to sit up.

He dropped the sandal he was holding and sank down beside her. 'I think it's a very good idea.' His mouth immediately claimed hers, while he lifted her up slightly so that he could wrap his arms about her and draw her up to him.

'Nick,' she began, when she had a chance. 'All that talk about marriage ... I'm not that easily fooled, believe me.'

'I want to marry you,' he answered, 'and be warned, I always get what I want.'

'I can't understand this. You want to marry me, and yet you don't love me. Somewhere, Barbro still wears your ring, so will you please let go of me?' When she tried to break away from him, he held her firm.

'I love every part of you,' he said. 'Isn't that enough? I'll go on loving every part of you.' His hand went beneath her skirt and up to the waistband of the slippery satin slip she was wearing, and she shivered as it went to her breast, cupping it before he bent his lips and kissed it through the material of her dress.

Kristen was overcome by the feelings he was arousing in her, and as he transferred his lips to hers, she began concentrating on their mouths and what his was doing to hers, and, in turn, what hers was doing to his. Once again, his hands explored her breasts, caressing them, and his body, against her own, told her he was aroused. She managed to push him away, and when she could speak she said, 'I may earn good money and drive around in a Mazda and have an expense account, but I've never been made love to. You've got this all wrong.' She could not prevent herself from sounding like a fearful small girl.

Her skirt and her slip were up about her tanned thighs and Nick was stroking her legs. At first, she was appalled by the recklessness of her response, and then she didn't care. She wanted him to touch her everywhere, and with a burst of pure passion, she clung to him and allowed herself to be carried away. Caught up in the turmoil of her desire, she did not want to stop Nick and so shatter these beautiful fragile moments.

For the first time in her life she was becoming utterly out of control and willing to give herself, and when Nick cursed and rolled off the sofa, in one movement, she had no idea why. Her wits lay about her like the scattered petals of the hibiscus by the pool.

'What's the matter?' she murmured.

'The matter is—someone is ringing the door chimes,' Nick said shortly.

Somewhere along the line he had removed her dress and the satin slip and he lifted these from the carpet, along with her shoes, and bundled them into her arms. Immediately, she had the strength to sit up.

'Take these to the guest powder-room,' he said, and she felt like some trashy call-girl caught by the man's wife.

While she was in the attractive, wallpapered room she heard voices and was sure they were coming from Frank and Donna Prentice, and then she was quite certain. Frank was saying, 'A Happy New Year, Nick. We were on our way home from the Royal when we decided to drive past your house. We decided that if there were lights on, we'd come up, but if the house was in darkness we'd go home.'

'I'm—glad you came.' Nick's voice sounded strained and, riddled with nervous tension, Kristen found herself giggling.

'Happy New Year,' said Donna. 'Sorry we don't have a lump of coal.'

'We—that is, Kristen and I—are not long back from the Scarlet Ibis.' Nick's voice was far too casual. 'She'll be through in a moment, I should imagine.'

'Oh . . . is Barbro still away, then?' Donna's voice, on the other hand, seemed to contain shocked surprise.

'Yes—apparently.' Nick was offhand now. 'She's still in the mountains with Jerry Ward—so I've been informed, anyway.'

There was a small silence and then Frank said, 'I'm getting the picture.' He laughed shortly. 'If you can't beat 'em, join 'em! I know Elizabeth has told you, of course. I've had a lot of hassles, believe me, Nick. She wouldn't listen.'

'Do you think I'd be the type to——' Nick broke off and when he continued Kristen thought he sounded angry. 'You can't seriously believe that . . .?'

There was more conversation, quieter now, and Kristen tried not to eavesdrop. She concentrated on dressing, making up her face and combing her hair. Feeling almost sick with humiliation at being caught here with Nick about two in the morning, she went through to the hall and then down the steps to the lounge.

Nick, she noticed, rigid with tension, had put on his shirt and his eyes met hers.

'Kristen,' he said quietly, 'you've met Donna and Frank.'

'Yes.' She tried to smile easily. 'A Happy New Year to you both.'

She tensed as they both wished her the same and froze at the coolness in their eyes. Particularly, she noticed the sudden tightening of Frank's face and the hard line of his lips. Of course, she told herself, they were still puzzled about Nick and Barbro. Well, so was *she*, for that matter. Resentment flared up within her. Frank Prentice appeared—as he had done on the night of the party at his house—strangely menacing.

'Let me get you something to drink,' Nick was saying. 'Or would you prefer coffee?'

Donna smiled a meaningless smile, in which there was no warmth. 'No—really! Thanks all the same. It's terribly late, after all.' Her remark was pointed. 'We just took a chance—and came in to wish you the season's greetings. We didn't know you had company. Do forgive us. Frank, darling, are you ready?'

'Sure.' Precise and impeccably suited, Frank glanced at Kristen. 'I can hardly say good night—it is, after all, as Donna remarked a moment ago, very late.'

Donna's laugh, in the background, was brittle.

'There's not much room in that courtyard, especially when two or more cars are parked there. I'll guide you out. Besides, I want a quick word with you, Frank,' said Nick.

Donna's perfume lingered in the air. Kristen remained standing and shaking, then she made an impatient gesture. 'To hell with them!' she whispered fiercely, but she was left feeling ruffled and upset.

When the phone began chirping she ignored it, waiting for Nick to come back, then after a moment or two she picked it up hesitantly.

'Hello?'

The line seemed to be quite dead, so she said again, 'Hello?'

'What number is that, please?' It was a girl's voice and the line was faint.

'Just a moment.' Kristen took the receiver away from her ear while she peered down at the number on Nick's phone, then she repeated this number to the caller.

'In other words, I *am* through to Nick Lathbury's house?'

'Yes.' A part of Kristen's mind was immediately on guard. She glanced towards the hall, willing Nick to come back into the house.

'You wouldn't be—Kristen—would you?'

Kristen's breathing was so uneven that she couldn't speak for a moment, then she said, 'Well, yes . . . but . . .' Suddenly everything began to fall into pattern and she felt her heart twist before it seemed to turn over.

'This is Barbro—but I'm sure you must have guessed. Where's Nick?'

'I'll—I'll call him.' Kristen tried to keep her voice carefully modulated.

'No, please don't bother.' There was a sarcastic edge to the voice. 'I wouldn't want to get him out of—bed, after all.' There was a slight pause, then Barbro drawled, 'So Nick is entertaining Miss Elizabeth Lathbury's expensive hobby? How very interesting! Tell me, how is the heiress? Still on the prowl, quite obviously. I don't know why I bothered to ask.'

Kristen felt a sudden cold shock, then her face went blank and she was too confused to think coherently.

'Are you referring—I mean—do you mean *me*? Could you please get to the point? I just don't get this.'

'I think you know what I'm getting at, but in any case, your relationship with Nick's aunt has been more successful than you can possibly imagine,' said Barbro. 'Elizabeth Lathbury has gone a bit further than just plying you with expensive gifts, Miss Ashton. You see—and she went to considerable effort to tell me this herself—if Miss Lathbury had to die tomorrow, you would be a very wealthy young woman. Isn't that nice? I believe that, since learning about his aunt's devious activities, Nick has taken things remarkably well. I think you know what I mean . . .'

There was a click as Barbro replaced the receiver and when Kristen looked up Nick had come back and was standing looking at her. His blue eyes went to the receiver in her hand and, as she put it down, she said, 'Barbro. That was—Barbro!'

'Barbro can go to hell,' he said swiftly. 'Like the Prentices.'

'Tell me, what's going on?' Kristen's voice seemed to be coming from a long distance. She swallowed and pushed her hair back from her face. 'Barbro says Holly . . .' Her voice petered out and she felt like fainting. 'I just don't believe this . . . She told me about the Will!'

Nick came over to where she was standing and took her by the shoulders. 'Listen,' he said, 'I've reached the stage—well, I reached it some time ago, actually—when I want to forget this whole mess.'

'Three things stand out in my mind,' she said, 'no—four. One, you called me a con-woman. Two, Frank Prentice doesn't like me—but then he happens to be Holly's *lawyer*. Three, Frank said, I couldn't help overhearing, "if you can't beat 'em—join 'em". Four and this one is very, very important, so listen carefully—Barbro said, and I repeat, "I believe that, since learning about his aunt's devious activities, Nick has taken things *remarkably* well". Now, I would go along with that. After all, *you* were very devious when you asked me to marry you, weren't you? In other words, if you can't beat 'em, join 'em. Take your hands off me!' She lifted her hands and grabbed Nick's arms and shoved them away from her. 'You're so sure you have the answer to everything. Damned cheek—damned, bloody cheek!' Her voice broke. 'How dare you, and how dare your aunt involve me in this affair?'

'Kristen, Barbro and I have been just about washed up for some time now. In fact, right at this moment she's with some——'

'Don't try to pull the wool over my eyes! On the night you arrived you spoke sharply to Holly when she criticised Barbro and called her "that girl". You said—that girl happens to be the girl you were engaged to, or the girl you were going to marry—something like that.'

'Well, naturally I did. I was still hoping to get things together between us.'

'*That* was before you knew about the Will—let's face it. Oh, you're very clever! Another thing, I refuse to feel guilty about this. I refuse to feel guilty about something I've played no part in. I didn't know what Holly was up to, and the gifts I've received from her have caused me nothing but—but embarrassment.'

Feeling utterly disorientated, Kristen rushed back to the bathroom, where she stood shaking and holding on to the marble top of the vanity.

'Kristen!' Nick was at the door and she opened her

mouth to say something, but the words, whatever she had intended them to be, just died in her throat.

After a moment she went to the door. Her golden-green eyes were wide with outrage. 'Take me home,' she said, then bent down to retrieve the hibiscus flower from the wastepaper basket, 'and take this!' Without stopping to think she threw the crushed bloom at Nick's face, then she pulled Holly's ring of garnets and pearls from her finger and hurled that at him as well, feeling shock as she saw it hit his check, causing an immediate welt there. 'After all,' she went on, 'it *is* an heirloom, and it's just about driven you out of your mind ever since you first saw it on my finger. Well, I'm giving it to you *now*, and you can explain to Holly in any way you choose. So I'm on the prowl again, am I? According to Barbro, that is. Barbro's a bitch!'

'I know she's a bitch,' answered Nick. 'I've been finding that out for myself.'

'She's gone out of her way to hurt Holly!'

'I know that, believe me. I tried to turn a deaf ear to Holly, but it became obvious——'

'She's hurt you. Right? She cleared off to the mountains for Christmas and the New Year when she thought you weren't going to make it.' Devastated, Kristen hardly knew what she was saying.

'I'm not hurt, believe me,' he answered.

'You tricked me,' she said bitterly. 'I'm beginning to see what those snide remarks were all about now. You've been so nice to my aunt, Kristen, why not be nice to me? You never know, Kristen, it might just pay off. I could go on and on. You, Nick Lathbury, are despicable and I loathe you. In fact,' she took a shuddering breath, 'I—I loathed you on sight.'

'Really?' His mouth curved in a tight sarcastic smile.

'Yes, really.' She turned away, suddenly blinded by tears.

'Let's put it this way, Kristen.' Nick's voice was suddenly sneering. 'You certainly had me fooled. You were very nice about loathing me, weren't you?' The words were deliberately spaced. 'And I guess I don't have to enlarge on that, right?' His eyes went to the broken hibiscus bloom on the floor and she watched him as he bent down and picked it up. 'Crushed hibiscus flower and all. I guess it didn't get mangled for nothing, did it?'

Her eyes watched him as he aimed the flower at the marble bowl. 'As for the ring,' he went on as he retrieved that too, 'I'll leave you to do your own dirty work. If you don't want it, speak to the lady in question.'

He reached for her hand and, forcing her fingers to open for him, pressed the ring into her palm and crushed the fingers down over them. Kristen's unhappy eyes remained on his face, noticing the red mark on his cheek.

'Very few women would have dared to throw that knuckle-duster in my face and have got away with it.' His dark blue eyes were blazing now.

'To think that all the time you were trying to get me into bed with you, and with all your big talk of getting married, all you had in mind was a marriage of convenience. What you really had in mind was—the Will! Holly's ridiculous Will.' She brushed past him and went back into the lounge and he was after her like a shot.

'Kristen, believe it or not, vintage cars, heirloom

rings and Wills were the very last things on my mind while I was making love to you,' he told her and, at breaking point, she wanted desperately to believe him.

Her thoughts flounced to some of Holly's puzzling remarks. 'Of course,' Holly had said once, 'I simply *adore* my Impressionists. Tell me, how do *you* feel about them, Kristen?'

'Right from the beginning, almost—well, after your row with Holly when she'd obviously told you what she'd done—you began referring to me as a con-woman. I turned up at Salt Air just at the right time, didn't I? You were able to give vent to your feelings. Well, let me tell you—my job liberates me from enslavement to any form of conning.' Kristen felt sick with anger. 'Where did I put my bag?' She glanced around and seeing it on one of the chairs, went and picked it up. 'I'll see myself out.'

Nick immediately blocked her way and caught her wrist between his hard fingers. 'Do you realise what time it is?' he asked angrily. 'I brought you here and I'll take you back.' He stared at her for a long moment, then he said, 'I didn't intend it to end this way tonight, Kristen, believe me.'

'No, you intended it to end in bed, didn't you? I'd like to scratch your face to pieces, and that's a fact!' She dropped her bag and flew at him with animal-like ferocity, and he caught her wrists again and this time he held them firmly.

'One thing about it,' he told her, 'one *good* thing—is that when you make it up with your ex, you can hand your lovely body over in mint condition, unmarred by having had sex with me.' He released her wrists and she stood staring at him in despair.

The tension and fatigue of the day, for after all, she

had worked right up to the last minute, suddenly caught up with her, and she began to cry softly.

'Kristen!' Nick reached for her and she backed away.

She felt insane fury. 'Shut up! Leave me alone, you two-faced devil. Take me back home.'

'I'll take you back when I'm good and ready and not before!'

From behind her fingers she watched him as he went to pour himself a drink.

'By the way,' he said, coming back to where she had slumped on to one of the sofas, 'I don't react kindly to having things thrown at my face. Just remember that, for future reference.' The naked hostility in his blue eyes caused her to shout at him.

'To think that—just so you wouldn't miss out on the Lathbury trinkets, antiques, Colonial mansion, vintage car, you name it—you asked me to marry you! In other words, if you can't beat 'em, join 'em. Talk about *me* being a con . . . you're no better!'

'You would have suited me very well as a wife,' he said softly.

Kristen shook her head from side to side, furious beyond words, 'Do you think I care a damn about a lot of Impressionist paintings?' She was just saying whatever came into her mind.

'Ah, so you knew about the Impressionists, did you? Well, yes, according to what Holly had to tell me, they're to go to you—along with the house, silver snuffboxes and crystal rose bowls and other items too numerous to mention—the whole damned lot, in fact!'

'You must have the dear, noble Frank let you have a list of everything, Nick. I hope the list makes you sick!'

'Did you expect me to stand by and *agree* to my aunt changing her Will,' he went on, 'whereby a girl who had somehow, along with her brother, inveigled her way into her affections, stood to inherit things that have been in our family for generations?'

'Leave my brother out of this! He had nothing to do with it—expect to use Holly's car on his wedding day.'

'I don't want to talk about it,' Nick said furiously. 'Actually, I couldn't give a damn. What she's done means nothing to me now, and my initial reaction has left me feeling sick.'

'So it should!' In her present mood Kristen went on, 'Your aunt could have struggled to resist temptation, couldn't she? She didn't have to like me!' She wiped the tears from her cheeks and went on bitterly. 'Whatever I own, whatever I wear—I pay for myself. I've always paid for myself. I will go on paying for myself—I'm no con-artist, do you understand?'

Nick lifted his shoulders and his fingers went to the swollen welt on his cheek. 'Kristen,' his voice sounded weary, 'let's face it—you hooked her, just as you've succeeded in hooking me. I'm hooked, woman.' He went on looking at her. 'But don't ever do this to me again, will you?' He took his fingers away from his cheek and looked at them.

Kristen's eyes were haunted as she looked at his cheek and she glanced down at her finger where, once more, the garnets and pearls glowed and gleamed in the lamplight. The ring would go back to Holly in the very near future, she told herself.

'I'm going to attend to this *thing* on my cheek,' said Nick, 'and then I'll drive you home.'

She watched him as he left the lounge, then on the spur of the moment, she lifted his car keys from the low glass and brass coffee table where he had left them and, standing up, got her bag and went outside to his car, which was parked beneath the fading stars.

When she got back, Holly's part of the house was in darkness, and she parked Nick's Jaguar in the dirveway and made her way to her flat.

Holly had slipped a note under the hall door. It read, 'Happy New Year, dear. This is also to let you know that your brother Craig phoned from Cape Town. All is well and he and Libby wish you everything you wish yourself. You won't believe it, dear, but they phoned from a yacht! When they couldn't get you at home, they phoned here.'

The tension that had been building up since the time that Ferdi had gone to Gstaad and come back with a girl called Reba snapped and, aware of an awful coldness in her, Kristen ran to her bedroom and collapsed in a flood of tears.

The festive season, for her, had clattered to an end.

CHAPTER SEVEN

DIRECTLY she opened her eyes, Kristen measured the harm that Holly Lathbury had done her. Holly's bitterness towards Barbro had flourished like a rank weed and it had driven her to make ridiculous changes to her Will for disposition to be made of her property after her death.

As she lay against frilled polka-dot-strewn pillowslips, Kristen's face was an inverted triangle spreading upwards from a firm chin to her huge, unhappy eyes. How could she possibly tackle Holly on this sensitive matter? What was more, how could she tackle Holly on New Year's Day?

When the telephone began an incessant shrieking demand to be picked up, she felt her muscles tightening with tension. She slid from beneath the sheet and stood up, hoping the unwelcome shrieking would stop, but it didn't. Going through to the hall, she lifted the receiver and, shaking her tangled hair back from her face, said, 'Hello?'

'Kristen? Ferdi here.'

After a moment she said coldly, 'Have you called to wish me a very Happy New Year? If you have, you might as well have saved yourself a phone call.'

'Kristen, listen . . . I know how you feel, but please listen. Give me a break. Look, I've been a fool. It didn't take me long to find out that this girl merely used me to get a free air ticket to this country. In other words, it's all over. It's finished.'

'Oh, too bad, Ferdi. How ghastly you must be feeling, right now. So—you have every reason to believe I'll take you back, is that it?' She laughed bitterly. 'Well, that's beautiful, isn't it?'

'No, I don't have every reason to believe that. I didn't say that, did I? All I'm asking is for you to consider giving it a trial run. I've let you slip through my fingers and I've regretted it ever since.'

'Ever since—what?' Her voice was sarcastic. 'But maybe she'll take you back, Ferdi. Why don't you ask *her* for the trial run, as you call it?' She took a long breath and expelled it loudly. 'Only you would have the nerve to suggest this!'

'Darling,' his voice was pleading now, 'don't talk like that. Just give it thought, that's all I ask.'

'What did you have in mind?' she laughed harshly.

'I thought we could start by going to my folks' farm today.'

'Oh, really? So you think a trip to a farm in the mountains will soothe me and do the trick?'

'Don't sound so hard,' he said plaintively. 'It doesn't suit you.'

'Well, it is me, and I am hard. You've made me hard, but I'll tell you something that will surprise you. I will go to the farm with you, but for reasons of my own. In other words, I'm promising nothing. Take it or leave it. I want to get away from here today. You see, the day holds no challenge for me.'

'I feel challenged enough for the two of us. You're wonderful.' Ferdi sounded frankly amazed.

'Why? Because I've agreed to go?' Her voice was bitter, reflecting the way she felt.

'Spare me the sarcasm, Kristen. It's not like you, and you know it. What time shall I pick you up?'

'You mean, what time shall you pick me up, just as though nothing has happened? Well, let me see. In about an hour?'

'Do you have to work tomorrow?' he asked. 'Some firms are open, others aren't. I'm not working, as it happens.'

'Neither am I,' she told him.

'In that case, pack an overnight bag and I'll ring my mother and tell her we'll be staying over,' he said.

As she put the phone down Kristen found herself thinking despondently that although she had called Nick a two-faced devil, she was no better herself. She was about to use Ferdi just as Nick had used her.

She had no sooner replaced the receiver when the phone went again and she picked it up, half expecting to hear Craig's voice, but it was Nick.

'Thanks for swiping my Jag last night.' His voice was cutting. 'If it's not too much trouble, I'd like it back and what's more, I like it back soon.'

'I'm sorry,' she said, 'but I'm on my way out to the misty mauve mountains. I'm going with Ferdi ... like Barbro, in other words. You'll just have to make a plan about getting your car back.'

'The plan is, Kristen, that you will return it.' He laughed softly. 'How reckless you are! So you're on your way out to the mountains? Off with the old year and on with the new, in other words. Oh well, nothing about you shocks me any more, Kristen.'

'I'm not interested in your opinion of me,' she retorted, and put the receiver down. She found she was shaking, and when the phone rang again she ignored it and went to her room where she slipped into a robe, then went in search of Holly's driver, Micky Naidoo, who fortunately was in the garden. She arranged for him to drive Nick's Jaguar back to his house and insisted that Micky accept money for a taxi back.

By the time Ferdi arrived on the scene she was dressed and waiting. With his dark hair, brown eyes in a face with an almost Roman nose and his cleft chin, he looked every bit the playboy type, she found herself thinking with a shock. Their eyes met directly. How could I have imagined myself to be in love with him? she thought.

'Don't kiss me.' Her voice was sharp and her eyes were hard as she watched him draw back quickly.

'Okay, if that's the way you want it.' He had spoken easily enough, but she was quick to sense the tension behind his words and to note the angry flush which spread into his cheeks.

'It's the way I want it, so please keep it in mind.' Her golden-green eyes went on studying him from beneath the brim of a floppy black sun-hat.

When they were on the way he said, 'I want to explain ... I got carried away with this girl. It's not unusual. It happens all the time.'

'Oh, yes, I know. In all the best town house circles, in fact.' She adjusted her sunglasses beneath the brim of her hat. 'Why do you refer to her as—this girl?' she asked. 'For a while *this girl* was your mistress. Right?'

'Yes, I know, but she was also just a part of the wonderful excitement of being on holiday in the Alps. Let me try to explain—the ski-lifts, the ski-jumps, brightly coloured clothes and woollen caps ... all that sparkling snow on towering peaks, the firs, dazzling blue skies—skies that put ours to shame, I might add. You have to see it to believe it. I got carried away—it's as simple as that.' After a moment he added, as an afterthought, 'Look, I'm really sorry.'

'Oh, don't be.' Kristen turned to give him her most flashing, sarcastic smile. 'I'd hate to feel you're distressed on my account. You see, I got over it so quickly, it's unbelievable. I've written our engagement off as an experience.' Her voice was sharp with spite. She had not known she could be so spiteful, and the sudden knowledge shocked her.

'You're out to get even with me, Kristen.' Ferdi sounded angry.

'I'm here, aren't I? Just let's say, for today, you got your way.'

'And tomorrow is another day,' he replied hopefully.

They arrived at the farm just before lunch. As Ferdi's parents came out to the car to greet them, Kristen realised she had done the wrong thing by coming, and her guilt at what she was doing to these nice people caused her to feel sick. She experienced some very bad moments when Johanna Jaeger fussed over her, as she would a daughter, while Ferdi and his father looked on, putting in a word here and there.

Since Ferdi's mother had arranged to have New Year's dinner that night, lunch was a light and easy meal, and somehow, through tall iced drinks, jokes and conversation, things were made easier for Kristen. It was easier than she had hoped for, in fact.

The farmhouse was old, with a view of the mountains from the big veranda. Sitting in the warmth of the early-evening after the end of the meal, Ferdi seemed to regard Kristen with the indulgent air of a victor, which she bitterly resented but, under the circumstances, could do nothing about.

Time ran its inevitable course to the moment when Ferdi and Kristen had to leave the farm.

'I'm so glad Ferdi will be settling down soon,' Johanna said, glancing at Kristen's ringless finger. 'Ferdi tells me your ring is being cleaned. Well, just watch out they don't switch your diamond. It's been done before, believe me. You know,' she went on, 'Ferdi has always been such a roamer. We'd begun to think he would never settle down.' Her voice took on a marked intensity. 'His father was so cross when Ferdi wrote from Switzerland asking for money. We had to send it, of course, but he must pay it back. That's only fair, don't you think?'

The muscles in Kristen's throat seemed to constrict and she was aware of the disappointment that would follow when Ferdi would have to break the news to them that he was no longer engaged to be married.

On the way back to the coast Ferdi said, 'You're so preoccupied. I just can't get close to you.' He seemed to be choosing his words with care, but he spoke with an edge of aggression which maddened her.

'Might I ask what you expected? Exactly, Ferdi, what did you expect? I'll be frank with you, I'm afraid of ever falling in love again,' she told him.

'Oh, so you're out of love?' Kristen saw his knuckles go white as his hands clenched the steering wheel.

'Yes, I am. When you arrived at the airport with another girl, I was devastated.' Not quite, she thought guiltily, thinking of Nick Lathbury. 'Actually, I went a bit crazy, for a while.' The beach house Salt Air and silk flowers came to her mind where, like the flaunting scarlet cactus he had referred to, she had lost herself in the excitement of Nick's arms, even while she was telling her side of the story to Ferdi, her mind rebelled at having, indirectly, to admit that she had in fact gone a bit wild.

Ferdi took his hands from the wheel and shrugged his shoulders. 'Let's forgive and forget. We can start again.'

'There's not the slightest possibility of ever starting again. I shouldn't have gone to the farm with you. For that, I'm truly sorry. I don't want to hurt your parents, particularly your mother. I'm very fond of her.'

'This doesn't concern my mother, Kristen, it concerns us.' After a moment he said in a hard voice, 'You agreed to go along just to get your revenge, didn't you? You've more than made yourself clear.'

'Being vengeful isn't part of my make-up, believe it or not,' Kristen answered heatedly. 'Holly Lathbury is the one who plots revenge.' She regretted the words immediately.

'I don't give a damn about Holly Lathbury,' Ferdi said quickly. 'I never did like that old bag.'

'She doesn't like you either, as it happens—and don't refer to her as an old bag! She's a very attractive lady.'

By the time they got back to her flat Kristen was feeling very depressed. 'I'll say goodbye here,' she said, and then, before she quite knew what was happening, Ferdi bent over and kissed her on the mouth. 'Think it over,' he said.

Moving her head, she said, 'No. It's over, Ferdi.' She opened the door and stepped out of the car, and she did not look at him as he drove off.

She was in her kitchen, with its gleaming copper pots and pans and clustered ferns growing in baskets, when Holly arrived.

At a glance, Kristen knew that Holly was upset.

'I hope I'm not intruding, dear? I know you've just got home, but I was in the garden and just happened to see you were with that Ferdi man. I thought it was all over, Kristen? How could you go and get involved with him again? I'm terribly disappointed.'

Ignoring the remark, Kristen said, 'Come through and sit down, Holly. Of course you're not intruding.'

'I shouldn't stay,' Holly said, half-heartedly, before she sat down. 'I'm afraid I'm not very good company.' She put her ringed fingers to her temples.

'Oh? Is something wrong, Holly? You look . . . well, terrible, actually.' Kristen's voice was tight with apprehension.

'Yes, something has happened and I'm terribly distressed. There was a scene with Frank and Nick, today, at Frank's house. I've known Frank since he was a mere boy in a high school blazer and straw boater. His father was not only our lawyer, but also a family friend, and when he died and Frank followed in his footsteps, it was only natural that I transferred my affairs to Frank.' Holly spread her fingers. 'So tell me, Kristen, what could have been more natural for me to get Micky to drive me there today to wish both Frank and Donna the compliments of the season? I mean,' she lifted her shoulders, 'I've done this sort of thing for years. I used to visit his parents. Well, I'd never have gone if I'd known that girl Barbro was going to be there. They're very close, you know. Barbro was their designer. What they see in her, I just don't know. She's a very unscrupulous girl—but then she had Nick deceived. I say *had*, because they've fallen out, I believe. In fact, Barbro accused *me* of helping to break their engagement.'

'Holly, let me make you some tea,' Kristen cut in. 'You're going to make yourself ill.'

'I am ill, Kristen. That girl has got a lot to answer for, believe me. Nick, is so self-willed—do you think he wouldn't have married her, if he'd wanted to?'

'Holly, maybe Barbro considered it best to be honest with you . . . about Nick, I mean.'

'Honest with me? Honest? In Barbro's case, Kristen, honesty, as you call it, is just an outlet for her vicious cruelty. To get on with my story, Frank had the nerve to phone for Nick—behind my back, of course. So . . . we all had some things to get off our minds, believe me. It's left me quite shattered!'

Kristen bit her lip, then she said in a soft voice, 'I've—er—had some very unsettling news . . .'

'Not Craig and Libby?' Holly's eyes widened.

'No—but can't you guess?'

Holly was plainly thrown. 'Who told you?'

'Never mind who told me. I've just found out that you've changed your Will, leaving your house, and many of your treasures in it, to a perfect stranger.' Kristen took a long shuddering breath.

'Not a perfect stranger, child. To a girl I've grown very, very fond of. A girl I know will take good care of these things.' Holly's face was stricken. It was also flushed and her blue eyes were beginning to blaze.

'Anyway, it's pointless now, since they're no longer engaged, from what you tell me. You must change it back to how it was—immediately!' Kristen was openly hostile now. 'You know, Holly, it was a mistake to meddle in Nick's love-life. Don't you see? You've provoked Barbro into saying all the things she said. Maybe she didn't mean them. I don't mean to be unkind.'

'Meddling!' Holly almost groaned. 'My dear child, I was not meddling. Tell me, what was I expected to do when I saw my nephew making a complete mess of his life by becoming engaged to that hard little schemer? Imagine a rash of ugly town houses on this magnificent site. Imagine my treasures being sold because *she* didn't like them! That lovely old car—she couldn't wait to get her hands on that, but what for? For a joke, that's what for. Anyway, Frank had the audacity to phone for Nick to come and take me home—because, I'd told Micky to come back for me at five. "Take your aunt home," he said, "before she has a stroke." A stroke . . . I ask you!'

'This is all so—bizarre,' sighed Kristen. 'You have years and years ahead of you, Holly. You're being *morbid.*'

'Bizarre, you call it? Morbid? Let me tell you, child, there'll come a time in your own life when you'll want to get your affairs in order.' Holly's hand went to her chest.

'Barbro is cruel with people,' she went on. 'She would have been cruel with Nick. It takes an aunt to see that, whether she happens to be an eccentric old spinster or not. Oh, yes . . . I know I'm referred to as an eccentric old spinster behind my back.'

'But that was no reason to leave your house and treasures to a stranger, Holly.' Kristen's emotions were in an uproar. 'I've been dreading having to approach you about this. That's why I went away with Ferdi. I feel quite shattered.

'I'm so angry about today,' Holly said. 'I'm so furious with everybody—that Will stands—and that is that.'

Kristen's knees seemed to give way and she sank to

the carpet. 'Holly, no! I won't let you do this to me. How dare you—you—use me?'

'I'm not using you, you foolish girl!'

Kristen stood up, in one fluid movement. 'I'm going to marry Ferdi,' she said. 'You're back where you started now, aren't you?'

'You'll be throwing your life away if you marry that man. Like a lot of men, he's utterly contemptible.' Holly was trying to get to her feet.

'Your opinion of Ferdi doesn't interest me.' Kristen decided to be cruel as she lied about Ferdi. 'You're being ridiculous. Just because you were jilted, all those years ago, there was no need to go through life with nothing but contempt for men—even your own nephew!'

Holly sucked in her breath. 'I feel most unwell,' she said. 'Please help me out of this low sofa, Kristen. I want to leave.' Her voice was suddenly very tired.

'Please don't look so devastated,' Kristen said worriedly. 'Holly?'

'I am devastated, child. What else did you expect, when you attack me like this—when they have *all* attacked me today?'

Holly's visit left Kristen feeling emotionally drained and she toyed with the idea of phoning Craig to ask him to come to Durban so that he could reason with Holly.

She had just showered and changed into fresh jeans and a loose pink sweater which was soft and fluffy, when the phone went. She answered it and her face went white when she heard the urgency in Holly's strangled voice.

'Come through quickly, Kristen! I'm—in—trouble.'

Holly was stretched out on her bed and Kristen was

shocked to see her looking so ashen, whereas she had been so pink in the face a short while ago. Holly's pulse was weak, but she did not seem to be in much pain as Kristen helped her into a more comfortable position and then, fumbling with the phone, rang Nick.

'Nick,' she said calmly, not wanting to alarm him, 'I need your help. Could you come as soon as possible?'

'What's wrong with Ferdi?' She heard the hard coolness in his voice. 'Why not ask him, since you've just been away with him?'

When he put the phone down on her, Kristen stood there, wide-eyed and horrified, and lost no time in getting through to him again. After what seemed like a lifetime, he answered and she could hear his growing anger.

'Nick, listen to me.' She tried to control her own anger. 'Just save your verbal abuse for another time. This call is very urgent, and it happens to concern your aunt.'

'What's wrong with her?' She was aware of the sudden tension in his voice.

'She's in a state of collapse, that's what. I think it could be a heart attack, but then I'm no doctor. She's not in pain, but certain symptoms are there.'

She heard him groan, then he said despairingly, 'Oh, God, no!' After a moment he said, 'I'll be there just as soon as I can. In the meantime, phone for an ambulance. The number is always kept in a diary next to her bed. It's a little oriental-silk thing—crimson. From this end—before I leave—I'll arrange to have her doctor waiting at the hospital. In any case, I should be with you before the ambulance arrives.'

Later, as she waited for Nick, Kristen began to feel real fear as she watched Holly.

'Don't let her die,' she prayed. 'Please, don't let her die!'

The moment she heard Nick's car she hurried to the door, then watched, with wide eyes, as he came towards her. If she had expected to see compassion or understanding there, for what she had gone through over Holly, she was in for a disappointment.

'Don't waste time trying to explain,' he said. 'I think I know what all this is about.'

'I've done all I can,' her voice dropped to a whisper. 'I've also packed a bag with nightdresses, dressing-gown, toothbrush and so on. Oh, I wish the ambulance would hurry up!'

On his way through to Holly's room he asked, 'How is she now?'

'Much the same. She'd been to see me only a short time—before ... She was in such a state when she arrived. I added to it, I'm sorry to say.' She blinked and bit her lip.

'Nick?' Holly opened her eyes immediately.

'I'm here,' he said. 'Don't worry, we'll soon have you with Dr Hunter. Just try to relax.'

'We only have each other,' Holly said faintly.

'I know.' His voice was gentle, as he took her hand. 'I know that.'

'Maybe I take advantage of that sometimes.' Holly sighed and turned her head restlessly.

'We both do.' He patted her hand and lifted it to his lips.

'Frank must be there at the hospital when I arrive. I have—things to arrange. I can't go on like this. I've upset this child. She's terribly distressed.'

'Don't worry,' said Nick, 'everything is going to be okay.'

'Okay?' A momentary glint of anger came into Holly's blue eyes. 'Everything with the young people today is either okay or—no problem. What's okay, Nick? What's no problem? Oh my, I've punished you. I've punished this poor unsuspecting girl. I've refused to talk—I've refused to listen.'

'Forget about everything. Just think about yourself, for the moment, and try to keep calm,' Nick told her.

Things were confused after the ambulance arrived. Kristen wanted to go with Holly in the ambulance, but the Sister in attendance insisted that there was no need to.

After the ambulance had gone Nick asked, 'Do you still want to come?' She saw a brief flicker of concern cross his face, before it turned back to a cold mask.

'Of course. I won't rest, otherwise. I was mixed up in this ghastly affair. I also played a part in upsetting the poor darling.' To her horror, she felt the sting of tears and glanced away quickly.

In the car she said, 'I don't know how I'm going to sleep in that house tonight, after what's happened.' They were in heavy traffic now, and the sun had already set.

'There are other things to think about at the moment,' Nick answered abruptly. 'Stop feeling sorry for yourself.'

'No—instead let's feel sorry for *you*, Nick!' Her voice was harsh. 'We'll think about what *you* stand to lose if—God forbid—Holly dies before Frank can change this hideous Will. How do you think I'm feeling right now?'

'I can always contest the Will,' he said cruelly. 'Just leave it at that.'

'You've treated me as one would treat a common

criminal,' she said, making no effort to conceal the fact that she was crying.

There was no softening in Nick's attitude. 'I don't want to go on with this useless discussion! I happen to be worried about her—nothing else matters.'

She willed herself to remain silent, while she waited for the hurt to subside. Nick was driving fast—recklessly, in fact—but suddenly he slackened speed. Turning to look at her he said, 'You might as well know this—I fell for you the moment I saw you. It runs in the family, apparently. First Holly and then me.'

In a small voice Kristen said, 'I don't know how to handle it when you're like this.' She felt exhausted and drained, and her beautiful golden-green eyes were full of suffering.

They had reached the hospital, on the Berea, and they stood about, waiting on Dr Hunter for news of Holly. The waiting seemed to go on and on.

Considering everything, the news was very favourable, but Dr Hunter went to considerable lengths to explain that Holly was now in intensive care and that later, she would need as much rest as she could get and a nurse to care for her when she went back home. He also asked to speak to Nick, in private, and when Nick got back to Kristen he said, 'Frank has put Holly's mind at rest. Everything has been attended to. She got Frank to write this little note—her own words, of course.' He passed it to her and, reluctantly, she took it and began to read. 'Nick dear, I wish I'd done all this with a better heart. It was, in fact, done out of spite—not a good thing. The Lathburys are—*and always were*—a lot of things, but they were never spiteful. Forgive your old aunt, will you?'

'She's not allowed visitors,' Nick was saying. 'The hospital will keep in touch.' His voice was soft, but the words had force behind them. 'This is over and done with, Kristen. Is that clear? We're not going to talk about this any more.'

Directly they got into his Jaguar she began to cry again and, when he took her hand, she pulled it away.

'You—and your bloody, catty Barbro!' she said brokenly. 'I don't usually swear, but I seem to have done nothing but, since I met you.'

'I don't look back,' he answered quietly. 'Who is this Barbro?' He started the car and drove her back to the flat.

'Get some things together,' he said, on the way, 'you'll be spending the next couple of nights at my place—in the guest-room.'

Holly's maid had turned on the lights, but Kristen's flat was in darkness.

'I feel shattered,' Kristen said, not moving.

'So do I,' answered Nick, 'but if the knowledge will make you feel better, Holly and I were fighting long, long before you came on the scene. Nevertheless, there's always been a strong degree of affection and mutual respect between us—no matter what's happened in the past.'

Listening to him, Kristen was shattered by the burdens Holly had created for herself—and everybody she was in contact with.

'Now that I know she's going to be . . . to come out of this—I'll stay in my own flat,' she said, after a moment.

'Don't argue.' He bent over her and opened the door for her. Get your things together.'

In the darkness, beside him, as they walked towards

her door she said, 'I'm going to start looking out for a new flat.' She shook her head. 'I—just can't go on staying here. I'm going to start packing tomorrow.'

'When did you last have anything to eat?' he asked, completely ignoring her remark.

She tried to think. 'I had—let me think—breakfast, before I left the farm this morning.'

'And you've had nothing since?' He sounded angry.

'No.'

'Well, I have an excellent casserole—just waiting to be popped into the microwave oven. If you feel like watching a video film afterwards, to take your mind off everything—well, there's that, too.'

'Right now, Nick, it seems easier to go along with you. I'm really exhausted, when I come to think of it.'

While she attended to those things that needed her attention, Nick went to tell Holly's maid what had happened, so that she would know what to do, and by the time he got back, Kristen was locking the door to her flat.

'Were you really serious about the casserole,' she asked, on the way to his house, 'or was that just an excuse to get me to come?' Suddenly, while she was speaking, she felt a surge of pleasurable anticipation when she thought of eating something hot and tasty.

'My aged housekeeper is a superb cook,' he said, 'I, on the other hand, am a wizard when it comes to cooking, or heating, what she's prepared for me in advance. A microwave oven takes up very little time.'

He had, Kristen noticed when they arrived, acquired more plants, and there were new urns, filled with pink and red geraniums, which were placed against the wall on the stairs to the carved entrance hall door.

It was wonderful to sink into one of the comfortable sofas, and while she was alone she gazed about the room. In many ways, she found herself thinking, Nick's taste was very much like her own.

After a few moments, she got up and went through to the well-appointed kitchen and, pushing her hair back with both hands, she said, 'Can I help you?' Her eyes met his and there was a short silence.

'I made it clear that I wanted you to relax,' he answered, and she felt a sudden elation that he should be concerned about her, after all.

When he phoned the hospital her heart began to clamour, but the clamouring subsided when he came back with the news that Holly was comfortable and in no danger. She closed her eyes in relief.

Although this was not the first meal they had eaten together, it felt like the first.

'I notice you've stopped wearing the ring,' Nick commented.

'I've put it away—until Holly is well enough to talk to about it. I don't want to hurt her.' She went on looking at him, then she said, in a small voice, 'You've been so insulting. Your—lovemaking—was nothing but an insult.'

'There was nothing insulting about wanting to make love to you, Kristen. I still do.'

'You were even prepared to marry me—because of the changes Holly made to her Will.'

'Look,' he sounded furious now, 'let's put one thing on record: if Holly had told me that she had decided to leave everything she possessed to the S.P.C.A. I would have said, "Fine, if that's what you want, that's just fine with me". But I wasn't prepared to allow some smart red-haired con-woman to get to work on her. It looked to me like you were on the make. I'm sorry, but there you are. I was also in love with you. I wanted to marry you, regardless.'

'And, once married to me, you would have set about punishing me, wouldn't you? What a callous thing to do!' Kristen felt fury surging right through her. 'I had a narrow escape! Believe me, Nick,' she went on, wanting to hurt him, 'you're the very last man I'd want to marry—and you can put *that* on record too!'

'Talking about being callous,' he answered, 'it would appear that all the time you were swooning with desire in my arms, you were, in fact, thinking of Ferdi.'

As soon as they had eaten she said, 'I'd like to go back to my flat. I'd rather not stay here with you.'

'Fine,' he shrugged. 'I can't force you, after all.'

They drove back to Holly's house without talking.

'I'll see you inside,' said Nick.

'There's no need to.' Her voice was stiff.

'Don't argue,' he retorted. 'I think you're being stupid to stay here tonight, but if you want to be morbid—be morbid.'

'I am not being morbid,' she answered. 'I'm used to being on my own.'

'Earlier on, you said you wondered how you could face being alone tonight, or have you forgotten?'

'Well, I was upset, but now I know Holly's going to be all right, I feel differently. Thank you for the dinner,' she added. 'It was very thoughtful of you and I enjoyed it.'

She had unlocked the door to her entrance hall and at that moment, there was a crash from the vicinity of the lounge. Kristen caught her breath, then watched Nick as he moved quickly past her and almost collided with Holly's Siamese cat, Nefertiti. The yowls of the cat caused them both to laugh, and Kristen said, 'She must have jumped through an open window.'

On further investigation she said, 'Oh, no! Look at my precious Lalique vase! I saved for four months to buy that!'

'I'll buy you another,' Nick said carelessly. 'Don't worry about it.'

'I can live without it,' she answered coolly, thinking of Barbro's insulting remarks about Holly's expensive gifts to her. 'It was nothing to do with you.' She was close to breaking point and thought—if he touches me, I'll scream. Suddenly, he closed the distance between them and took her into his arms.

'Leave me alone,' she said quickly. 'I told you how I feel about you. Why don't you listen?'

'Did you really expect me to believe that?' He gave her a searching look before his lips came down on her own.

Struggling against him, she said, 'I prefer not to be reminded of what's happened between us.'

'I intend to remind you,' he muttered.

At first there was violence in his kiss, then he took his mouth away before he kissed her again, longer this time, deeply and lingeringly. Kristen felt her lips responding tremulously and her limbs felt suddenly drained of strength.

Nick held her away from him so that he could slip his hands beneath her loose pink sweater and as he stroked her breasts, they responded to his touch immediately, like small rosebuds, unfurling their petals for him. She found herself straining against him, wanting more, and their mutual desire began to mount, tearing down the barriers which had sprung up between them. Nick's hands went round to her back and he stroked it with long, sensuous strokes which ended up on the soft curves of her bottom. He led her over to one of the sofas and pushed her down, then lay down beside her, drawing her close to his body. Kristen felt a surge of erotic sensation that left her reeling, and she knew she wanted Nick Lathbury as she would never want any other man.

When he kissed her on the lips again, she kissed him back and found herself being swept up in the eager curiosity of sensual pleasure. She longed to unbutton his shirt and to kiss his chest, but she resisted the longing and her arms went to his shoulders, drawing him nearer to her. Their bodies strained together. Nick drew his fingers through her dark red hair and caressed her neck, stroking her ear lobes languorously, and she thought she was going to melt away. Her control was slipping, but when the phone rang she was immediately on the alert and tried to break away from him, but he held her down, pressing his lips against her own. Moving her head from side to side, she managed to say, 'Nick, the phone.'

'Leave it!' he said angrily.

'No—don't you see? It could be urgent. It could be the hospital!' She used all her strength to push him away.

He swore softly. 'You're right, of course. What is it with me?'

She watched him with wide eyes while he went to answer it. She realised now that she had begun to meet Nick's desire head-on, with no thought of the aftermath.

'No,' Nick was saying, 'I don't mind if you *do* speak to your fiancée. Why should I? I see. Well, don't overdo it—never mind who I am. That, after all, has nothing to do with you . . .' There was a longish pause, then he said in a softly dangerous tone, 'Just don't count on it—you might just bite off more than you can chew.'

There was a look of anger on his handsome face as he held the receiver out to Kristen. Very deliberately he held her gaze as she got up to take it, then he said, 'Your boyfriend sounds the worse for wear—just more than a little drunk, in other words, and full of idle threats—but I guess that's your problem.'

Kristen's face was set. 'I don't want to talk to him.'

'Well, you come and explain that to him.' With an impatient movement he put the receiver down on the yellow-wood chest-of-drawers. 'I'll leave you to it. Thanks for a more than entertaining evening.'

'You've loved saying that, haven't you?' She shook her hair back from her cheeks. 'You'll go over and over it in your memory for a long time to come, won't you? I'm not going to apologise for the way I got carried away tonight, if that's what you're hoping for.' She brushed past him so that she could pick up the receiver and then, speaking in a furious voice, she said, 'I don't want to talk to you. Why did you ring me?' She was silent for a moment while Ferdi replied.

'I've lost my car keys, Kristen. Where the hell are they?'

'How should I know where they are?' she asked angrily. 'Look for them!'

As she put the receiver down she felt out of control of her life.

'Well, since this isn't exactly the Ice Age,' said Nick, 'I suppose it's common enough for one guy to walk out as the other walks in.'

'Stop being flip with me, Nick!' Kristen found herself shouting. 'That isn't the way it is with me.'

He considered her with cold eyes. 'No? Well, you could have fooled me.'

'What's it to you anyway?' she asked in a much softer voice. 'As usual, you were just using me to amuse yourself.'

'And you? What about you? Who exactly did you have in mind when you responded so willingly a few moments ago?'

'Oh, Nick!' She shook her head and turned away from him, then she swung round again. 'Please give me *some* credit. You just don't understand. You just don't want to understand. You condemned me from the beginning.' There was despair in her voice and she had been about to tell him she was in love with him, but stopped herself just in time.

'You never cease to amaze me,' he told her. 'I don't know what else I expected, to be quite honest. Good night. If you're nervous, being alone in this big house, you know where to find me.'

The phone shrilled again and she let it go on ringing and ringing, then she picked up the receiver and said angrily, 'Get off this line—and stop bothering me!'

'Kristen,' said Ferdi, 'I know I've had too much to drink, but I can explain . . . I went to this place——'

'I'm not interested in where you went—and now will you stop worrying me? The way I feel about you right now is that I'd like to strangle you! You've caused me nothing but trouble and unhappiness. You cause your own parents unhappiness, let alone me!' She slammed the receiver down and stood shaking.

After a while, she bathed and prepared for bed. Misery was beginning to go to work on her in earnest and she cried despairingly. For the first time in her life she was experiencing the profound upheaval of having really fallen in love. Day by day, since meeting Nick Lathbury, she had become possessed by her yearning to be loved by him—and to love.

She was awake at the first sign of a flaming sunrise which heralded a radiant day. The thought that she had to drive to a cosmetic factory in Johannesburg brought her a certain solace, because she would be away for four days—time enough in which to try to regain some of her composure.

After she had had breakfast, she telephoned the hospital and was told that Miss Elizabeth Lathbury had spent a comfortable night.

It was a perfect day for driving, calm and not too hot. Kristen left the coast behind, stopping only for coffee in one of the small midland towns where she also made arrangements, through Interflora, for flowers to be sent to Holly.

Feeling happier now, she went back to her car, which was parked nearby and shone in the warm glow of the sun.

Her time in Johannesburg was hectic, but she had been booked into a very expensive hotel where the walls of her huge double room were covered in pale apricot silk and the white ceiling was touched with gold. Her balcony overlooked a scented garden. The hotel was slightly out of town and at night, she could see the traffic lights streaking along the main artery which led directly into the city. After the strain of the past few days it was a relief to lose herself in the beautiful room at night. She should have felt very successful, but she didn't, as she brooded and tried to analyse her feelings towards Nick. Everything was wrong with her life, she found herself thinking.

Eventually her business trip, which had revolved

around jars of cream and bottles of lotion, drew to an end and it was time to pack and drive back to the coast, where she would arrive at the end of a long day and where she knew her problems still awaited her.

Holly was out of intensive care but still in the hospital and during her entire stay there, Kristen made sure she always arranged her visits when Nick would be at Lathbury Interiors. Since there was no need to consider Ferdi coming back into her life, she lost no time in clearing this issue with him. At first, he refused to be put off and sent her masses of Iceland poppies, with stems which seemed far too fragile to hold the giant blooms. One day he sent an ancient Egyptian bracelet of blue lotus flowers. The bracelet was promptly returned to him, along with the box of Art Nouveau stationery, which had come in the post. Gifts were contrary to Ferdi, and she had always been aware of the mean streak in him—unless generosity was aimed at himself.

Finally he lost interest, and she saw him having lunch one day, with a girl who was wearing the Egyptian bracelet.

CHAPTER EIGHT

At the end of the third week, and with a nurse in attendance, Holly Lathbury arrived home. Kristen was with her when Dr Hunter called to see her, stressing that Holly was to have complete rest, simmer down and stop worrying.

'What you need to discover, for yourself, Elizabeth, is peace and well-being.' His tone became bantering. 'Now, to be perfectly honest, you are *not* going to find this peace if you keep on meddling in the affairs of young people. Let young people get on with their affairs—their love-affairs, houses and modern life-styles. There's nothing much wrong with you, except your attitude to life . . . and I'm being perfectly candid with you. Now,' he held up a hand, 'don't get cross . . .'

Soon after Holly's return, Kristen decided to explain that she had been offered a position in Johannesburg and, as a result, wanted to go away by herself, to think things over.

'Oh, no, Kristen!' Holly's voice was filled with dismay. 'Do you know, I've felt twenty years younger since you've come to live in the flat. I'll be terribly upset if you leave.'

Confusion welled up in Kristen and she said, 'I just think it might be a good idea, Holly. As you know, my engagement is broken. It would mean a complete change of environment and it could be—you know . . .' she found herself floundering, 'stimulating.'

'Yes, I appreciate the urgency you might be feeling to get away, after what's happened here,' Holly answered quickly, 'but think very seriously about leaving. Where had you thought of going for your little holiday?'

'I haven't made up my mind. Maybe the Wild Coast.' Unable to meet Holly's probing blue eyes, Kristen looked away.

'Why don't you go along to Salt Air?' Holly asked. 'Think about it. It's vacant at the moment.'

And so, two days later, and with very mixed feelings, Kristen was on her way to Salt Air. She had bought enough food for her entire stay there and intended to have a breeze which, in this case, meant just that—soaking up the sun and enjoying the sea-breezes.

As she parked her car in the carport, however, she had the sensation of having been abandoned, and she tried to overcome the feeling as she carried her possessions into the house. The root stump of the fallen syringa tree helped to remind her of Nick. Someone had sawn off all the branches and cut the trunk into small logs. The logs were stacked near the white ornamental garden wall.

More and more memories of Nick began to haunt her, and she asked herself whether she had been a fool to come back to Surprise Bay.

The baskets and vases of realistic silk flowers created a mood of welcome, and yet her eyes rested on them moodily. Although there was a garden, there were no flower-beds. The garden, kept immaculate by the Indian caretaker, consisted of flowering shrubs, trees and sweeping lawns. The house was aired and cleaned by his wife, who also took care of the laundry after guests had left.

Kristen's attention was immediately drawn to a red-lacquered chest, which had not been in the house before. There were two Japanese Imari plates on top of this chest, and when she went to admire them she saw that the chest had been made in Korea. What a find! she found herself thinking. There was also, newly hung, an explosive modern painting in the bedroom with the potted palm, and, since Holly had been in the hospital, she found these additions to Salt Air puzzling. Perhaps Nick had been here again? Her heart gave a sudden jump. Perhaps these were gifts intended to surprise Holly when she was fit enough to visit the house?

Kristen had left her flat before sunrise and had arrived just on lunch-time, and after changing into an Indian cotton caftan in shades of apricot and blue and held up by narrow shoulder straps, she prepared lunch and, acting on an impulse, opened a half bottle of champagne, which sparkled invitingly in her glass.

Unlike her previous visit, the weather was perfect, so she took her lunch out to the long veranda which was glassed-in at either end but open to the sea along the front, from where the view of the scalloped fringe of the surf, as the breakers rolled over and beat down on to golden rippled sand, was breathtaking. Her caftan fluttered in the breeze and brushed against her body, causing her to feel—uselessly—aware of it.

Later, she spent the sun-drenched afternoon on the beach, which was warm and fragrant and reminded her, foolishly, of freshly-laundered sheets. Feeling suddenly refreshed, she stretched her arms upwards and shook her hair until it swirled about her face, then

she put her head back, enjoying the feel of the sun . . .
and trying not to think of Nick.

An Indian woman, wearing a brilliant scarlet-and-
gold sari and carrying a heavy basket of brass and
beaded curios, came towards her. The colour of the
sari created a dramatic contrast against the white-
spumed blue sea. Barefoot and graceful the woman's
feet made swimming movements in the sand as she
moved towards Kristen.

'I saw you from up above,' she said, pointing
towards Salt Air and the other beach houses in the
vicinity. 'I came down all those steps to show you
what I got. I have been from bungalow to bungalow,
but not many people buy today.' She laughed softly.
'Now tell me, you would like to buy, yes? It has been
a bad day for me. I have many children.' She dropped
to her knees in an easy and graceful movement. 'Very
nice brass here. Some Indian vases, beads—little
trinkets—look nice on you.' She lifted long lashes to
look at Kristen.

Delving into the basket the woman lifted out a brass
bowl and unwrapped the gauzy purple paper. 'I will
make a special price for you because I want to leave
for my home now.'

Kristen accepted the bowl and turned it round
between her slender fingers. Her oval-shaped finger
nails, which were pink-lacquered, looked stunning
against the gleaming brass.

'It's very heavy, isn't it?' she murmured. 'Heavy for
you to be carrying around, along with all the other
things in your basket.'

The woman tilted her sleek head backwards and
laughed lightly. 'Yes, it is heavy. That is why I ask you to
buy. I have much respect for brass things—and you?'

'Well, yes. I collect things like this, so I'll buy it.' Kristen reached for her beach-bag. 'That is, of course, if it's not too expensive?'

'It is cheap, and I make even cheaper for you.'

Buying the brass bowl had somehow uplifted her, and when she got back to the house she set it on the red-lacquered chest between the two Imari plates, then she went to shower and slipped back into the cotton caftan, which fell in folds to her feet.

She had brought a number of exiting new novels with her, not to mention several expensive magazines. She felt single and very uninvolved, and carefully shunned such articles as 'Looking For A Husband?' and 'You—And Your Sex Life'. Her eyes kept straying to the beach. It was late afternoon now and the beach, which was usually very quiet anyway, looked golden and empty. At least, here, Kristen told herself, there were no hassles and problems to worry about for a few days—no men in her life. She tried to convince herself that she felt languid and utterly at peace, and she thought about exciting clothes and exciting things she intended to buy for her flat, if she decided to go on staying there.

Later, because she felt restless, she poured herself a glass of chilled white wine and took it out to the veranda, trying to convince herself that she enjoyed being single, career-orientated, very uninvolved and successful. From where she was sitting she could see— at the far end of the veranda—the house next door. An elderly woman, wearing a floppy straw hat, even though the sun had just about gone, was working in the garden. She looked tanned and relaxed, with the problems of her love-life safely behind her. Her husband, tall, tanned and handsome, with silver hair, was obviously enjoying retirement, and Kristen watched him moodily, as he threw a ball for the dog to chase and then she heard him laugh. It was an easy, self-confident laugh—the laugh of a man who had retired from a top executive position and who did not have to explain himself. Would Nick be like that, one day? Somehow, she knew he would.

She had watched the sky grow dark and had eaten dinner and was trying to read when she heard someone at the glass doors, and then Nick's riveting voice called out, 'Kristen! It's Nick.'

Feeling almost weak at the knees, she pulled back the curtains and opened the doors. For a moment, neither of them spoke, and then, when they did speak, they both began to talk at the same time.

'Go on,' he said, his eyes searching her face.

'Holly told me that Salt Air was going to be empty.' Kristen tried to calm her thumping heart.

'Let's start with this,' he said, 'this house does not belong to Holly, it belongs to me, although she and her friends have always used it.'

She watched him as he lifted his belongings from the veranda and came into the room. She thought she was going to fall apart, and shivered.

'She should have told me that, right from the beginning. This explains how you knew the plates on the wall were Spode—when I asked you whether you knew. It explains why *you* bought the flower paintings for the house. Why didn't you tell me?'

'Well, I'm telling you now.' He spoke on a note of mockery.

They could hear the roar of the sea and then Kristen said, 'To think I've filled the whole house with stupid silk flowers! I feel an utter fool.'

'Don't be. I have no complaints about the flowers. Don't worry, I can live with the silk flowers.'

Glancing at his luggage, she said, 'Well, obviously, I must leave.' She brushed a strand of hair from her cheek and as she lifted her arm the bangles which she had also bought from the Indian woman on the spur of the moment before leaving the beach made soft jangling noises. Nick's handsomeness, she thought a little wildly, was almost intimidating.

'Why all the falling apart?' He gave her a long look. 'This house has accommodated the two of us before today, hasn't it?'

'That was different,' she said.

'Why was it different?' His dark blue eyes held hers.

'You know perfectly well why it was different. There was a cyclone going on out there in the Indian Ocean, that's why. We were stranded here together.'

'What time do you think you'd get back to your flat tonight? I left Lathbury Interiors and I've been hitting the breeze. It's a long hike. Don't be a little fool!' He sounded angry. 'Besides, I came here to talk to you. I want to clear things up between us.'

'Oh, you do?' Her voice was suddenly sarcastic. 'What do we have to clear up? Have you come to apologise for doubting me—without having given me the chance to defend myself?' She moved away from him. 'Oh, no, I'm not going through all that again, Nick. I'm leaving.'

When he caught her by the wrist, excitement ran along every nerve in her body. After a moment she said, 'I don't know what you have in mind, but isn't it always a mistake to try and recapture the past—for what that past is worth?'

'*For what it was worth*, Kristen, I asked you to marry me—and the offer still stands. Or have you forgotten?'

'I'd like to forget it!' she said. 'You used that as a lever to get me into bed with you. You also used it in an attempt to overcome certain legal matters, didn't you? To use Barbro's words to me on the phone, "if you can't beat 'em, join 'em". Or was it Frank's words the night he and Donna turned up to wish you a Happy New Year? I'm so confused by everything—I can't remember. So . . . all that has changed now.' At the risk of more hostility she went on, 'Legal matters no longer have to govern your behaviour towards me, in any way. I know I don't have go into detail regarding this very sensitive matter.'

She watched Nick as he went to pour himself a drink. He looked tired, she thought. He sighed as he looked about the room, then he asked, 'Who brought the brass bowl along? You?'

'I bought it on the beach today. I was going to leave it for Holly, but under the circumstances, I'll take it away.'

Nick put his glass down and loosened his tie and took it off, then he shrugged out of his jacket and threw it on to one of the sofas.

Watching him, Kristen said, 'You carry on as if you've just come home to the little woman. I resent that. I don't care what time I get back to Durban tonight—I'm leaving. What's more, I've been offered a position in Johannesburg, which I intend to accept. In other words, Holly's flat will be falling vacant in the very near future.'

As she made to walk in the direction of the

bedrooms, he came after her and, placing his hands on her shoulders, turned her round to face him.

'What did you expect me to do? Did you expect me to keep my jacket on and to stand around wearing a tie? I've come straight here from the office, and I intend to make myself comfortable.'

Kristen was shaken with nerves. 'I find this very embarrassing,' she said.

'Where's the embarrassment? We've shared some rather intimate moments in this house—or have you conveniently forgotten that too?'

A wave of longing swept over her, but she said, 'This is precisely what frightens me. You see, I don't want anything like that to happen again.'

'Why not?' He gave her a long look and their tension was suddenly like a taut wire.

Ignoring his question, she asked, 'Did you know I was here?' Her face was devoid of any make-up and her eyes looked huge in her face which already had turned a shade darker than the usual golden tan she had acquired during hours spent on the beach with Ferdi before he had gone to Switzerland.

'Yes.' Nick's eyes went over her face. 'I did know.'

'So is that why you came? You really did come to talk to me?'

'I've just told you that.'

Her mind flew to Holly. 'You were informed of my whereabouts, in other words?' He still had his hands on her shoulders and she moved away from him.

'What does it matter, Kristen, how I got to know you were here?'

'It matters a lot, actually. You and your aunt must think I'm a complete fool. So you came to try your luck with me again, did you?'

'I want to marry you,' he said. 'I intend to convince you that I mean it.'

After a long moment she said, 'I'm not in love with you. I told you that.'

'I don't believe you.' He held her eyes with his own. 'You don't believe it either.'

'What decided you that you were in love with me?' She spoke with a deliberate calm that was almost hostile.

'Let's put it on record—*again*. I was thrown the moment I bent down to look at you through the window of your red Mazda at the airport. I wasn't prepared for what I saw, believe me.'

After a moment he expelled a long impatient breath and ran his fingers around his chin. 'Let me tell you— I wanted you from the first moment I saw you. I want you now. Be prepared for that—and by want, I mean love!'

'So here *you* are, also like Kuan-Yin—but let's say, *god* and not goddess of mercy—expecting me to be madly grateful that you *are* here to climb into bed with me! But no doubt this suits your informal lifestyle. With a broken romance behind you, it doesn't really matter who you marry, does it?'

'You're deliberately misunderstanding me.' The expression on his face was hard.

'It wasn't a good idea for Holly to tell you I was here. Dr Hunter particularly told her to stop meddling in the lives of young people.'

'Kristen, contrary to what you—or Dr Hunter— may have to say or have in mind, I do not rely on Holly to dictate my lifestyle to me. In other words, I'm not one of Holly's possessions.'

'Yet you went to considerable effort to fight for

them, didn't you—when you thought you were going to lose them?' Her voice was bitter.

'Tell me,' there was a chill in his voice now, 'how would you have reacted—no, don't you walk away from me, Kristen—if things which had been in your family for generations had been suddenly signed over by an eccentric aunt to a beautiful red-haired girl who very feasibly, I think, could have been listed as a con-merchant. As I once told you, if she'd decided to leave everything she possessed to a cats' home or Boys' Town—I could have accepted that.'

'Some of the things you've said to me are unforgivable!' she hissed. 'I was completely unaware of what Holly had done—and yet, condemning me without evidence, you came up with such snide remarks as "You've been so nice to my aunt, Kristen, why not be nice to me? You never know, Kristen, it may pay off . . ." That sort of thing.' Her voice broke. 'I couldn't make you out. I *still* can't make you out, if it comes to that.'

Nick put his hands on her shoulders and she placed wide-spread fingers against his chest and tried to push him away. 'Don't touch me! I couldn't bear it.'

'Don't let's make heavy weather of this,' he answered, very softly. He lifted her hand and began to kiss her fingertips, while he went on looking at her with those astonishing blue eyes. 'I'll admit that, most of the time, I wanted to hurt you. I wanted to find out what made you tick—what was behind Holly's infatuation. Imagine, the one woman I've really ever loved in my life and I wanted to hurt you. Sometimes, I wanted to devastate you. I'm sorry.'

'You very nearly succeeded,' she confessed.

'Do you think you could love me?' he asked.

'No.' She closed her eyes.

'Yes.' His hands went to her shoulder-straps and he eased them over her shoulders; the caftan slithered to the floor and Kristen was left standing in her tiny briefs. She forced herself to go on standing there while his eyes roved over her. Tight with tension, her golden-green eyes brooded on his mouth, then she said in a furious voice, 'Everything you see before you was inherited and belongs to me and me only. I don't intend parting with it frivolously. How dare you do this to me. Nick?'

He went on looking at her. 'But you do intend to share this inheritance, I take it? With love—and being loved, in return?'

'One day, maybe!' Her voice rose and tears of indignation glistened in her lovely eyes. 'I don't intend ending up like poor Holly.' She crossed her slim arms over her breasts and added, 'Just because of some man!'

'I love you,' he said. 'It's time you got the message.'

'You have a strange way of showing it!'

Very deliberately, his arms closed about her. 'I don't think it's a strange way.' His voice was soft and unexpectedly gentle.

He moved his position and took his arms away so that he could free her arms, then he bent his head to kiss the cleft between her small breasts. He caressed her skin with his tongue and a surge of erotic excitement ran through her; each languid stroke was like a tiny bolt of lightning.

She was fully aware that Nick knew she was in love with him—that she was vulnerable, and when he kissed her, on the mouth, she tried to stifle the urge to part her lips for him, but, as she moaned softly, her arms went up to his shoulders and she put her head back, so that he might, in the end, kiss her deeper, as he gently probed between her lips. When he drew away from her abruptly, her eyes were baffled and questioning.

'Am I boring you?' he asked. 'I mean, you have gone to considerable lengths to express the opinion that you don't consider this to be part of love . . . something vitally important to a marriage, in other words?'

She felt her face go hot. 'You're—not—boring me,' she said. 'I love you, Nick.'

'Well, what is all this about?' Suddenly she was in his arms again and their mouths were meeting, their bodies straining together. Nick drew his fingers through her hair and stroked her ear lobes languorously, and she thought she was going to faint in his arms if he didn't *do* something. Her control continued to slip away.

'Darling,' he said softly, 'we've had a rough take-off.' He placed his hands against her cheeks and searched her face with a tender expression in his blue eyes. 'You're so beautiful, and I love you so very much.' He lifted her into his arms and carried her through to the bedroom.

As he kissed her, he stroked her arms and then one hand went to her flat stomach, just below her naval. Moving his position, he bent his mouth to her navel and explored it, gently before he gave his attention to her breasts again, while she continued to drown in sensation.

She longed for their bodies to be closer and looked up at him with impatience when he stopped.

'What are you looking at me like that for?' he asked. 'What are you thinking about?'

'I'm incapable of thinking,' she answered, after a confused moment, 'although I *should* be thinking, Nick.'

'What about?'

'I should be thinking about the golden rule for one thing.' She broke off and moved her body close to his again, searching for the wonderful warmth of him.

'And what golden rule would that be?' He began to stroke her hair and went on looking into her eyes.

'You know—being—untouched—until the wedding night. I know it's supposed to be old-fashioned—but still . . .'

There was an agonising pause on Nick's part, then he asked, 'Do you want to go by this rule?'

Casting fate to the winds, Kristen shook her head.

'Do you want to wait?' His eyes held hers.

'I can't,' she whispered, as mists rose out of the valleys, engulfing her, and a heady swirl of sensations caused her to cling to him. Every part of her longed for him.

'I love you so much, Nick. I just won't wear white, that's all. The veil of Brussels lace will have to wait for our—daughter, okay?'

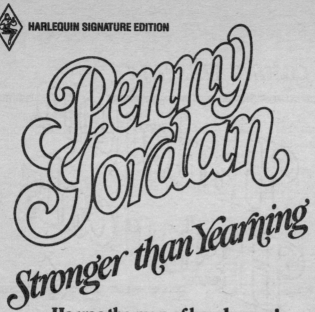

Penny Jordan

Stronger than Yearning

He was the man of her dreams!

The same dark hair, the same mocking eyes; it was as if the Regency rake of the portrait, the seducer of Jenna's dream, had come to life. Jenna, believing the last of the Deverils dead, was determined to buy the great old Yorkshire Hall—to claim it for her daughter, Lucy, and put to rest some of the painful memories of Lucy's birth. She had no way of knowing that a direct descendant of the black sheep Deveril even existed—or that James Allingham and his own powerful yearnings would disrupt her plan entirely.